THE FINAL TALES OF SHERLOCK HOLMES

(VOLUME TWO)

By

Dr. John H. Watson, M. D.,

as edited by John A. Little

Paperback ISBN 978-1-78092-791-6
ePub ISBN 978-1-78092-792-3
PDF ISBN 978-1-78092-793-0

Published in the UK by MX Publishing
335 Princess Park Manor, Royal Drive, London, N11 3GX
www.mxpublishing.com

Cover design by www.staunch.com

Contents

Foreword.

The story of how these late adventures of Holmes and Watson came to be discovered has already been related in Volume One of this collection. I repeat it now for those few who may have inadvertently missed the first book.

The building known to all Holmes afficionados as 221B Baker Street had fallen into such disrepair by 1955 – thanks to the efforts of the German Luftwaffe, and many years after the detecting duo had passed on – that the local authorities deemed it unfit for habitation. It had to be knocked down. By my father, as it happens.

Eneder Little had built up a successful business as a builder in London, having been forced to emigrate from Ireland after the lunatic DeValera's disastrous economic policies of the 1930s. His company (Motto: 'No Job Too Big For Little') was granted the contract to demolish nos 220A, 220B, 221A, 221B, 222A, 222B, 223A and 223B Baker Street and rebuild a terrace of spanking new luxury four-bedroomed town houses, complete with all modern conveniences.

Before the buildings were due to be levelled, he was examining the basement at 221B when he discovered a tall dust-covered office cabinet hidden in a corner behind a dilapidated kitchen dresser. Having no keys, my curious father grabbed his jemmy and cracked open the lock that controlled the four metal drawers. There was nothing but wrapping paper inside the top one, but the other three drawers revealed a series of packages of A4-sized spiral-back handwritten notebooks, each held together by two elastic bands in the shape of a cross. Never having read a book in his life apart from his annual accounts, he had no comprehension of his discovery. But he was a cautious man and decided to dump the lot into a cardboard box and take it home that night. And then promptly forgot all about them.

I became aware of this event when I was helping my mother and sister to clear out his effects the day after his funeral. He married late in life, and returned to live in Dublin towards the end of the 1970s with his wife and two small children.

I had climbed up a ladder into the attic and started handing down cartons of what was obviously rubbish – ancient account books from his building company, newspapers, magazines, old clothes, sporting equipment from his hockey and cricket-playing days – when I discovered a cardboard box, covered by some spare fibreglass insulation. Its bottom was lodged firmly between two beams and pulling it out almost caused my foot to slip off the beam and crash through the bathroom ceiling.

A rapid inventory produced sixteen packages, each of which contained a varying (one to nine) number of A4 notebooks dated from 1925-1930. Later, when we were sitting down, exhausted after our day's work and with our shared grief, I asked my mother about them and she told me what little she could recall of their origin at 221B Baker Street. I pulled off the elastic band and opened the first notebook of a package marked February 1925, the earliest period. Intriguingly, it showed a faded red stamp with the tiny word 'Strand' repeated around the edges, and 'REJECT' in large letters diagonally across the middle. It was in surprisingly good condition, for a manuscript that had lain in its cardboard coffin for over eighty years.

I had only to finish a single chapter to realise what I held in my hand. All my life I had been a great fan of Holmes and Watson, and had read their exploits avidly, once when I was a teenager, and again when I had been hospitalised for a week while some varicose veins were being stripped. After a quick check of all the packages, it became clear that we had in our possession one novella-length and fifteen shorter adventures of the Baker Street detectives in the last years of their lives, all of which had been rejected for publication by Strand Magazine for a variety of reasons. One of them pitted the pair against the evil witch of Clapham Junction. Others treated pornography, rape and necrophilia. These were dark subjects for their time, but it occurred to me that Conan Doyle's later pre-occupation with all things supernatural – caused by the loss of his wife and son – may have been a factor in the rejection of the final detective stories, which, as everybody knows, should always have a rational solution, with no hint of smoke and mirrors, magic acts or spiritualism.

As I read on through that dark night, I understood why the first story had never been published within their lifetime. It concerned a series of quite appalling serial murders that, in the London of 1925, would most certainly have caused public mayhem and a possible breakdown of society, had it been fully reported in the press, or if Holmes and Watson had not finally solved the case. After a small amount of editing by me to smooth out Dr. Watson's archaic style, this story has now been published as a separate novella within '*The Final Tales Of Sherlock Holmes – Volume One*', entitled '*Sherlock Holmes And The Musical Murders*'.

Volume Two, which I trust you are about to read, contains the first selection of the shorter works, also suitably edited.

John A. Little,
Portobello,
Dublin,
Ireland.
March 8th, 2015.

2.   Sherlock Holmes And The Hampstead Ponies.

'Do you know, Watson. My late brother had quite a fondness for this dish.'

For a brief second I imagined that my dear old comrade-in-arms, Sherlock Holmes, was about to display something I had never witnessed before. Emotion. But the moment passed, as I realised he was examining his Weiner Schnitzel with the eyes of the world's first consulting detective, and finding that something was, indeed, rotten in the state of England.

'Waiter!'

We were celebrating my birthday with a late supper in Simpsons-In-The-Strand, having spent the early part of the evening guffawing at Buster Keaton's hilarious antics in 'Sherlock Jr.', cinematic evidence that my friend's fame was now truly international.

It had been some time since the dreadful murders of Sherlock's brother and father, events that brought us back together after almost twenty years apart. The case had revealed certain details about Holmes' childhood which helped to explain his ambivalent attitude towards members of the opposite sex. Details that my companion had refused to discuss openly with me, a decision I had willingly accepted. After all, any close friendship between two human beings need not involve complete disclosure about everything in their past. And ours was a covenant, just like that between David and Jonathan in the Book of Samuel. It did not depend upon a selfish end.

I had hoped that further adventures might ensue, but the six months since February had provided precious few problems for Holmes to get his teeth into, apart from the well-publicised but quite simple affair of the bungled theft of the Greenwich Observatory Shepherd Gate Twenty-four hour clock. At least he had broken his cocaine habit, and seemed content in his old age – in early August of 1925 he was an extremely fit grey-haired seventy-one, whereas I was now an overweight white-haired dodderer of seventy-three – to study the latest developments in his field, and to relax by composing and playing his violin music, reading, walking around London and attending the latest concerts and silent motion pictures. His moods no longer vacillated in accordance with his level of boredom. Yet he still did not suffer fools gladly.

'Waiter!'

A pimply youth scurried through the buzzing dining-area to our table.

'Yes, s-s-sir? Is s-s-something wrong?'

'Weiner Schnitzel should be made with veal. This is pork.'

Holmes handed his plate to the stuttering waiter.

'I'm ... s-s-sorry, Mr Holmes. We've r-r-run out of veal. Most c-customers don't m-m-mind pork. Can I r-r-replace it w-w-with s-some other dish?'

'I'll have the stroganoff, provided it's real beef.'

'Y-yes, s-s-sir.'

'Excellent. I perceive that you are new to your job, cannot whistle, have poor hearing, are studying to be a chef during the day, have no siblings and just one parent, an overly-protective mother. You should dab those pimples with horseradish sauce for fifteen minutes. Also I suggest you start reading books out loud to yourself. It'll teach you how to breathe properly and may even cure your stammer,' Holmes finished kindly, if somewhat loftily.

The waiter backed away in horror at Holmes' uncanny revelations, obviously worried at the thought of having to read books.

'Holmes. The things you do know,' I murmured.

'You see, Watso ...'

'... but I do not observe. The distinction is clear. Just put me out of my misery. Tell me how you did it.'

'Elementary. You know my method. I have trained myself to see what other people overlook. He is our buxom housekeeper's first cousin, and she told me all about him this afternoon, when she heard we were dining here.'

'Hah! Perfectly simple, as usual.'

Holmes sat back in his seat, grinning broadly at his little joke.

'But the cures for pimples and stuttering ...?' I queried.

'... are my own. I looked them up in my medical dictionary before coming out. That's me. Sherlock Sr., the crime-crushing criminologist, at your service. Remember the rules of detection, Watson, according to Buster Keaton. *One*: Search everybody. *Two*: Look for a clue. *Three*: Shadow your man closely.'

I had not fully adjusted to my colleague's glittering new personality since he had returned to London from his long sojourn in a Sussex apiary. He claimed it was the result of a regular diet of Royal Jelly, and that his research into the bees' product had enabled him to distil a serum to slow down his aging process. He had even persuaded me to take the foul stuff. Sometimes I found his lustre a trifle annoying and almost wished that he would return to his usual morose self. Even take to the cocaine needle again. Little did I realise how soon my wish would come true.

'Do start without me, Watson.'

'Thank you, Holmes.' I already had.

'As you know, I'm normally not that bothered about food. Perhaps my fussiness has something to do with the absence of a decent case to absorb my interest. My mind simply rebels at stagnation. I need work. A problem to solve is all I ask. Where are the murderers, thieves, kidnappers and blackmailers of today? Are they in jail? Have they all retired? Has Scotland Yard improved its service to the public? I doubt that. Is it not strange, Watson, that my profession, the profession *I* invented, is now depicted humourously in the cinema for all to see, and that there are at least two other consulting detectives at work in London, competing with me for clients?'

'Really? Who are they?' This was a game we played from time to time.

'That appalling Belgian, Poirot, with his waxed moustache and his insufferable little grey cells, and the oh-so-delicate Lord Peter Wimsey, with his crass money and title. They might be getting all the best cases. Someone with a really difficult problem might be mounting their stairs at this very moment.'

'They are not in your class, Holmes,' I suggested loyally, between mouthfuls.

'I agree. But youth is on their side. And we are getting on in years. There. I said it before you had to, Watson.'

He lapsed into a moody silence after this familiar exchange. Soon I noticed the acned waiter had begun to edge nervously through the noisy crowd towards our table again.

'M-m-mister Holmes. T-telephone f-f-for you.'

Holmes leapt up eagerly and followed Lily Hudson's cousin out to the foyer. I grabbed the opportunity to finish off my splendid roast partridge in cider, with leeks and smoked bacon. I believe it was George Herbert, that undervalued English poet, who wrote that living well was the best revenge. He hit the nail right on the head. As neither Holmes nor I had been blessed with children, we could afford the little luxuries of old age, fine food and wine being of paramount importance to me.

I had just completed my repast when Holmes returned, all fuss and bother.

'Come, Watson. That was young Lestrade. Rather desperate, I fear. He needs our help. We must away to Hampstead.'

'Why?' I enquired petulantly. I had been planning some dessert. Crème brûlée, perhaps?

'Because, old fellow, they have found the dead body of a baby girl in some bushes on the Heath.'

'And what is so unusual about that, may I ask? Modern women are forever leaving their unwanted babies up there. And their illegal back street aborted foetuses. Young people today have no morals, no decency, no ... sense of responsibility.'

'Yes, yes. But normally the child would have a head. Hurry up, Watson. Let us go. The game's afoot. Never mind your bull pup. My persuader will protect us both. You have finished your meal, have you not?'

Holmes was sunk in a private reverie as our hansom cab creaked and swayed through the dense, humid fog towards Hampstead Heath, his mood altered by the possibility of an interesting case. What kind of fiend would chop the head off a baby, for God's sake? Thank heavens he had finally come around to my way of thinking and agreed to eschew the murderous modern Beardmore taxi and the dreaded underground with its noisome carcinogenic smoke, in favour of the old reliable growler. Slowly but surely we clipped and clopped our way through the twilit evening.

He sat opposite me, eyes closed, lips compressed, fingers steepled beneath his chin. People who did not know him would imagine that he was sleeping. Anything but. His febrile mind would be churning over all possible explanations of a headless baby, dumped in a wood. I knew better than to disturb him.

This taciturn behaviour continued as we dismounted from the brougham at the end of the East Heath Road and hurried down to where a section was cordoned off, near the Vale Of Health. This part of London had not yet been electrified, so the gas lamps could still fizz and sputter their eerie welcome at us. Torches flickered brightly through the mist to illuminate a few uniformed policemen and the agitated, ferret-faced son of Holmes' old enemy.

'Where is it?' demanded Holmes, with not so much as a how-de-do. 'And who found it?'

'Thank God. Over there.' Jasper Lestrade pointed to a gap in some bushes. 'It ... *she*, was found by some kids, about three hours ago. They are being comforted by their parents. The body was hidden beneath some loose branches. We have taken photographs and are searching within a radius of one hundred yards for any sign of the ... remainder. And before you ask, that set of puncheons was laid to avoid contamination of footprints. Oh, and this was found tied around the infant's ankle. I have no idea what it means.'

Lestrade handed over a short piece of red string to Holmes, who looked at it briefly with interest, before returning it.

'Yes, yes. I know what this is. I will explain later. And you may have to search the entire Heath for the head. Needless to say, without it we may find it difficult to identify the corpse. Come, Watson.'

'Here, Mr. Holmes. Use my torch,' offered Lestrade.

'Thank you. I might want to talk to those children later. Hah! The little darlings will think twice about playing on Hampstead Heath in future, eh, Watson?' Holmes muttered under his breath.

I followed my colleague across the puncheon and into the holly bushes, where a tiny bundle had been covered with a blue police jacket. He bent down, hesitated, then swiftly yanked it off.

By the size of its trunk, I estimated the poor naked mite to have been at least six months old when it died. Whilst I found it difficult to look at the gap on its shoulders, Holmes whipped out his pocket lens and was examining the spongy severed area in close detail, even sniffing it. When I finally plucked up enough courage, with a sickened heart I could see that the head had not actually been chopped off, with a blade of some kind. It had obviously been *torn* off when it was still alive, as though two sets of people were playing a game of tug of war with the unfortunate infant. I prayed God it was not a mother and father.

'Most interesting', murmured Holmes.

'I ... I must go.' I do not believe my friend heard my muttered words as I turned and limped back hurriedly over the puncheons and into another set of bushes, where I politely and swiftly deposited my entire evening meal, in reverse order, the bird before the soup. Normally I have a strong stomach, which had been seasoned by the ghastly horrors of the second Anglo-Afghan War all those years ago, but tonight it simply revolted. A baby! With her little head ripped off! In London! What on earth was the world coming to?

I planted myself groggily upon a bollard near Lestrade and massaged my aching leg, which still contained the remnants of a bullet fired into it by an Afghan jezailchi at the disastrous Battle of Maiwand in 1880. No doubt Holmes would appear soon with a full explanation of everything. Yet I fancied this case might flummox even his superb mind, with its powers of abduction and ability to infer the truth from an incomplete set of facts. As Holmes had suggested, with the head, the child might be identified. Without it, we were lost, unless some parent turned up, looking for their infant, an event by no means certain in London of 1925. And fingerprint records would not include those of an innocent baby.

My negative thoughts were interrupted by Holmes himself, who edged his way backwards slowly along the plank on his knees, his lens fixed lovingly to the adjacent grass, like a hungry bloodhound on the scent. We could almost hear him slavering.

'Gentlemen,' he said, eventually standing up. 'These are treacherous waters indeed. Has there been a circus or a carnival show of some kind on the Heath recently? One that might feature a horse, or horses?'

'Not that I know of,' replied Lestrade. 'But I will find out.'

'What do you think, Holmes?' I asked. 'That a horse knocked off her poor little head?'

'Watson, I never surmise without the full facts, as you very well know. It is a capital mistake to theorise before we have all the evidence. There are unmistakable signs of at least one horseshoe on the ground near this child. Its head was probably ripped off from behind by a ferocious blow, without it knowing what was happening. The fact that its corpse was hidden under branches so soon after death obviously suggests murder, rather than an accident. Judging by the internal damage to the vertebral and carotid arteries within the remaining neck region, the child had probably suffered a stroke, or hemoplegia as it is called by Watson's august profession. Such paralysis is rare, and to my knowledge has been documented only by Sigmund Freud, as long ago as 1887. That might be the reason ... *she* was killed. The red string is a Romanichal custom, whereby newly-born babies wear it around their ankle for the first year of life, as a sign of respect for the blood of the new mother, who is worshipped for her creative power. Hence, carnival, circus, travelling camps. The baby is ... or was, a Roma. A gypsy. That is all.'

'That's quite enough, Holmes. And it is of some relief,' I muttered, standing up, stunned as usual by Holmes' gifts.

'I'll keep a couple of men here, to look for the other remains,' said Lestrade, all business now. 'We'll also check for any horse-riding that might occur along here, although the bridal paths are on the far side of the Heath. I think I might establish whether any other parks in London have had carnivals recently. I'll also put a man on checking the Register of Births in the London area from four to eight months ago. But I suspect gypsies don't bother with such niceties. And I suppose there'll have to be an autopsy. Will you be at Baker Street tomorrow morning, if I call?'

'Indeed we shall. I don't believe that we have that much scheduled for tomorrow, do we, Watson?'

It was obvious to me that this attempt at humour was a simple camoflage by Holmes, to hide a deeper emotion aroused by the sight of the wretched infant and her fate. I knew that he needed to control his feelings in this way, to enable him to concentrate his mind on the problem at hand. How did the child die? Why? Who or what killed her? Who was she?

That was when it happened. A scene which has replayed itself over and over again in my mind ever since, awake or asleep, and made me wish that I had brought my Webley revolver with me. I am a practical, yet God-fearing man, but I never imagined that I would some day witness an event that seemed beyond all rational explanation, a supernatural nightmare.

The quartet of riderless ponies came at us out of the mist like the ghostly Four Horsemen Of The Apocalypse, an impressive motion picture by the Irishman Rex Ingram that we had recently enjoyed. The hooves of conquest, war, famine and death clattered at a gallop along the cobble stones of the Vale Of Health. Their ears lay flat and puffs of pearly breath whistled through their flared nostrils. We three stood transfixed with shock, awaiting our destinies beneath their iron shoes. Believe me when I tell you that I genuinely thought I was due to meet my darling wives Mary and Bea in heaven again that very night.

Then they were past us as suddenly as they had appeared, veering left into the dense, swirling haze of the Heath, towards the village itself. They were followed by two young men jogging down the Vale, one of whom had a black, heavy-looking rectangular box hoisted upon his right shoulder, with one eye clamped to it, and his hand rapidly winding a crank.

'Who the bloody hell are you? And what are you ... doing here? Goddamm it! You've ... ruined the shot.'

The accent was American, as was the quite exceptional rudeness. It came from a gigantic overweight figure with a shock of red hair and a grotesque unlit cigar protruding from the corner of his mouth, like a brown stick of Brighton rock. His shirt glistened with sweat and he was gasping for breath.

Holmes was the first to recover, as Lestrade and I stood frozen in the aftermath of the ponies' charge.

'I am Sherlock Holmes and this is my colleague and good friend Dr. Watson. And over here is Inspector Lestrade of Scotland Yard. And you, my good sir, are trespassing upon a crime scene.'

'A crime scene? And what's the crime? Stopping a film from being made when the Heath has been leased to me at great cost for the night? That's a goddamn crime, for sure!'

The unmannerly yank and his cohort had come to a halt by the bollard.

'I would like to know your name,' said Holmes quietly. 'And I would also like to know more about your ponies. They are white Welsh cobs, are they not?'

The pair of filmmakers seemed to realise that they might not hold all the trump cards in this particular scene, and after a quick, knowing shake of his head from the cameraman to the rude American, decided to become more compliant. The second man laid his recording box gently down on the cobblestones. He was slim, bald, suntanned and elegantly attired in a safari outfit. His stone face and cold, starey eyes reminded me eerily of Buster Keaton, but without a single trace of humour.

'Yes, they are Welsh cobs,' he said, in pure Oxford tones. 'I must apologise for my colleague, gentlemen. We are having a trying day. I am Leonard David, the director of '*My Dream Of Ponies*', a children's film. And this aggressive fat person is Sheldon Welles, the film's producer. It is his money I play around with, so he might have good reason to be angry. What is the nature of the crime, may I enquire?'

'A six-month-old baby girl has had her head removed,' replied Holmes pleasantly.

'Good God!' The two men might have rehearsed their response to this news, it was so completely harmonious. Yet it seemed doubtful to me that they could know anything about this crime. I imagined that all they were interested in was making motion pictures, and the enormous profits that came from doing so.

'Have you been in full control of your ponies all day?' enquired Holmes. 'It is possible that a horse or pony kicked the child's head off. As an accident, of course.'

Welles' eyes narrowed, as though he sensed a familiar threat of a legal nature, one that might damage his pocket.

'Aw, now,' he cried, plucking his cigar from his mouth. 'You sure can't lay that one on us. We have a handler for the hosses, and they're damn well trained. Why, I'll bet they've returned straight back to him at Well Walk. Ain't that right, Lenny?'

'Yes, Sheldon. It is. Calm down. You are not in danger of being sued. I believe we can help you, gentlemen. We hired the four ponies from a local carnival at the fairground site over in Pryors Field. The handler came with them. Frankly we may have to do the same tomorrow, if I cannot edit you folk out of tonight's scene. It has to be shot in twilight, you see. With the gas lighting. It is a dream sequence,' the director finished off rather lamely.

Fairground. Carnival. Ponies. Roma. Holmes was obviously on the right track. All we had to do now was go over there and challenge them to identify their missing child. But for some reason he had different ideas.

'Right,' said Holmes abruptly. 'Change of plan, Lestrade. As the carnival will still be on, with people all over the place, and Watson seems a bit fagged, we will meet in Pryors Field tomorrow at 10 am sharp. Maybe you could arrange to interview the pony handler with these two gentlemen now. Were they let out for a run on the Heath this afternoon, for instance? Also check the hooves for any sign of blood. I suspect that you will not find any, yet it must be done.'

He turned to me, ignoring the muttered protests of the filmmakers.

'Watson, I don't believe that we can achieve anything further tonight, and as I have not yet eaten, perhaps you would care to join me for a libation at a nearby hostelry. Jack Straw's Castle is but a short walk from here. Hopefully they can also put us up for the night.'

I did not need a second invitation for a strong whiskey and soda to settle my grumbling, newly-voided stomach, even though I was anything but a 'bit fagged'. We set off briskly towards the inn while Lestrade obediently led the reluctant Welles and David after the ponies and up towards Hampstead Village.

The following morning found Holmes and I strolling down East Heath Road and into Pryors Field, neither of us particularly refreshed after a fitful night in unfamiliar beds. I had dreamed that I was riding Cervantes, my faithful old war horse, up the Khyber Pass, being chased by a herd of elephants, each of which was being driven by an identical baby with a red lasso twirling around its headless body. I had woken several times during the night in a feverish sweat, and was only too glad to rise early and doze in a tepid bath for an hour before joining Holmes for breakfast. He appeared not to have slept at all, or even changed his attire. The excellent bacon and eggs held no interest for him. How his habits altered when he was presented with a problem to solve!

The London particular had cleared and it was a bright morning with a clear blue sky overhead. The first signs of an early autumn were evident with an occasional falling leaf. Our pace quickened when we noticed that the carnival rides and tents of the Macaroni Brothers were being dismantled.

'We must hurry. They are preparing to leave, Holmes,' I said.

'Watson, you do have a talent for stating the obvious,' he replied tetchily, and somewhat unnecessarily, I thought. Why couldn't he just sleep like everybody else?

The field echoed to the clang of metal upon metal and the repetitive splat of wooden planks being laid one on top of another. About thirty men were hard at work, breaking up a huge roller-coaster, a pleasure wheel, a multi-coloured carousel, a children's galloper, a wheel-of-fortune, bumper cars, the usual chair-o-planes, cake walks, steam yachts, a high striker, tents, slides and shy-stands. Even a tunnel of love and small ghost train. I could see no white ponies, although several brown dray horses were being used to haul the heavier items. Strangely, I could see no women or children. The workers consciously ignored us, as well as Lestrade, who was already in place, talking to a miniscule old character with a red scarf around his neck, who sat on the ornately studded stoop of Madame Oracle's brightly-coloured wagon. His brown face resembled a road map of the British Isles, it was so deeply grooved and coarse. Oddly, he looked for all the world like a leprechaun, complete with green stove-pipe hat, as he smoked his corncob pipe contentedly.

'Any sign of a head yet?' Holmes interrupted Lestrade's conversation rudely.

'Ah, Mr. Holmes, there you are. No. Not yet. My men are searching the entire heath at this moment. Let me introduce you to Tony Macaroni, the owner of the carnival. I have explained our discovery and questioned him about missing children, but he does not know of any among his troupe.'

Holmes nodded briefly at Macaroni, before continuing to address Lestrade. 'What about the four white ponies? Did you examine them? Any blood on the hooves?'

'No. And they were corralled all day until that scene last night.'

'I thought not,' muttered Holmes. He turned and looked at the gypsies dismantling their rides, his swift, piercing gaze absorbing the entire panorama in a split second. 'Inspector Lestrade. Firstly, I suggest that you keep this story out of the papers for the time being. Secondly, are you happy with the departure of this carnival from the location of a possible murder? You must explain to them that they cannot leave this site until the baby has been identified and its demise fully explained. You might be letting a murderer or murderess off the hook. At the least, a terrible accident may have occurred. All of the carnival's equipment must be forensically examined for blood stains, and the entire site searched for the child's head. Chop, chop.'

Lestrade stood up abruptly, as though his Commanding Officer had upbraided him for not following an order. Jasper Lestrade was the complete antithesis of his incompetent, scornful father, happily now pushing up daisies in Highgate Cemetery. The younger man, being ambitious, understood that Holmes was capable of solving the crimes that he could not, and knew that his career would benefit from the great detective's influence. The fact that he was in love with our housekeeper Lily, Mrs Hudson's niece, who unfortunately returned that feeling with interest, was something my aged body had recently learned to accept. After all, the pleasures of the flesh for us chaps must come to an end at some time. I had to accept that there would never be a third Mrs Watson. But I digress.

'We have to scapa flow (*go*) to Dover to catch the late 'a penny dip (*ship*) to Calais, mister,' muttered the pretend leprechaun, his unlikely estuary English and cockney rhyming slang carrying within it more than a hint of aggression. 'And we're supposed to be all set up again in a Noah's Ark (*park*) outside Paris by late afternoon. It's the first stop on our European tour. Else there'll be a lot of disappointed French tea pot lids (*kids*) there tomorrow night.'

'Then disappointed the lids will just have to be, Mr Macaroni,' snapped Lestrade, clearly furious at being reminded of his duties. 'Mr. Holmes is correct. My men will need to carry out their work over the next few hours, and then return to searching the heath afterwards, if necessary. Can you please order your people to refrain from putting things away, and ask them to stand by for interview by me?'

'Watson will assist you with the interviews, Lestrade, while I have a look around the site,' stated Holmes. 'It is all right, Mr. Macaroni, you do not have to join me.'

Holmes was already on his way towards the squat base of a dismantled galloper, magnifying lens clutched fiercely in hand. The exotic pony rides lay still on their sides in a ring upon the grass, like a giant magic circle, eerily devoid of their electric motor.

'Is this the entire camp?' I addressed the leprechaun. 'Where are the women and children?'

Macaroni stepped down off the stoop.

'Scapa flowed a'ead. Yesterday.'

He shook his head sadly, as though he'd seen it all before – *yet more police prejudice against us poor travelling folk and gypsies* – and limped over towards the men, dragging a gammy right leg behind him that looked far more damaged than my limb. Only then did I realise that he was a small man, a dwarf, as some people called them. Rather unkindly, I thought. Poor chap! I watched him from the corner of one eye while he gathered his men around and imparted the bad news.

Lestrade hurried off to reschedule the new business at hand. I decided to spend the time applying Holmes' rules of observation around the site. Not knowing much about them, I was interested in how these nomadic people lived, where they slept, ate and bathed! I had read somewhere that it was a completely patriarchal culture. Roma women were considered clean, or *wuzho* from the waste up, but impure, or *marime*, from the waste down. While they could happily wander around topless, they were forced to cover the bottom half of their body completely with wide skirts and avoid any casual contact with the opposite sex, due to the group's antiquated ideas about personal hygiene. Well, really! What kind of a retrograde society would regard the purity of the delightful fair sex as in any way suspect?

My idle curiosity led me to the steps of the fortune-teller's wagon vacated by Tony Macaroni. Were they not called *vardoes*? What was it like inside, I wondered? And who was Madame Oracle?

A beaded string curtain dripped limply down the entrance. I pushed it aside and bent my head to avoid a low wooden ceiling. Despite the sunny day outside, it was almost pitch black inside the caravan, and I could see nothing.

'Tell your fortune, sir?'

The startlingly deep voice came from the rear of the van. Far from the traditional old crone with a scarf around her hair and a ball globe in front of her, as my eyes adjusted to the dim light from the door I realised that Madame Oracle was a beautiful pale-faced young woman, with long, thickly-braided black hair and a strong Eastern European accent. Beautiful, heavy-breasted, obviously pregnant and shockingly bearded. A rich full Abraham Lincoln hung from her chin like a vandal's drawing on an oil painting. She was sitting on a bunk in the elaborately decorated cabin, like on a berth aboard ship, with a table in front of her, playing out a pack of cards on top of a large chart. I could see they were Tarot cards, and that the chart showed their meanings. I imagined what Holmes would think of this, knowing how sceptical he was of all things non-scientific and unknowable. He would have laughed, and I might have joined him. But why not? In for a penny, in for a pound. I would have to make an effort to keep my eyes off that beard, though.

'It shouldn't take you very long,' I joked, sliding onto the seat opposite her.

She laughed throatily. 'You first cross hand with silver.'

'Oh, well, of course.' Penny, my foot. I dug a florin out of a pocket and passed it over to her. She pressed her thick, sensuous lips over the coin as she bit down hard on it.

'We will see what cards say about mysterious snow-haired man with white moustache. Past, present, or future?'

'Eh, the future. I'm quite familiar with the others, thank you.'

She moved the deck across the table to me.

'Shuffle,' she said.

Now shuffling a deck was never my forte, not having played much at cards, despite each of my wives attempting to teach me the contract bridge Acol bidding system, which I abhorred. But I did the best I could, and handed them back to her outstretched bejeweled hand, thinking that a random selection of such cards could hardly have any real value to a person's life, other than a highly superstitious one. Obviously a different story must be told after each shuffle.

She dealt the first card slowly off the top of the deck. It showed a well-dressed gentleman showering coins on a pair of beggars.

'Ah, Six Of Pent...acles.'

'Is that good?' I asked.

She consulted her chart. 'It mean you upright man and solv...ent in material affairs. You have charity, symp...athy and kind heart. You Lord Of Ma...terial Success.'

That sounded good, if a trifle excessive. I grinned at her to show how accurate her reading was. She turned over the next card. It was upside down.

'It is the Wheel Of Fortune, ill-dig...nified.'

'Good grief, that sounds terrible,' I said.

'It is,' she said, matter-of-factly. 'You have bad luck. Do not bet on horse races. Diffi...culties lie ahead. There will be delays to enter...prises.'

'Oh, do go on.' What enterprises? My practice was almost non-existent. I had hardly any patients now, and the only business I was involved in was helping Holmes solve his few remaining cases. She palmed the third card out.

'It is Queen Of Wands. We ignore that.' She placed it to one side and dealt another card. 'The Four Of Wands. The Lord Of Per...fected Work. Also ill-dig...nified.'

'What does it mean?' I asked.

She read slowly from the chart, fingering her beard. English was obviously not her first language. 'That you rely on cer...ceremony, routine, order; that your life ruled by strong values; there will be a period of res...respite before you can con...clude a project.'

Really? That could apply to anybody, I thought.

The next card was the Knight Of Cups, upside down. She placed it beside the Queen Of Wands.

'We also not use that.'

'But why not?' I enquired.

'Because it say you are trickster, em...bezzler and liar, who has trouble dis...cerning the end of truth and beginning of false...hood.'

'I say! Steady on! How dare you!' I stood up abruptly. Madame Oracle was getting out of hand. I was about to leave in high dudgeon when she revealed yet another of her damn cards very quickly. It was an inverted picture, this time of a seated devil, complete with goat's head and hooves. I knew who he was, right enough.

'It is the Lord Of The Gates Of Matter, ill-dig...nified. It represents true evil. You are am...bitious, greedy, lustful and in bon...dage to another person.'

'Great heavens. This is too much. I am leaving, young lady. Do you know something? That beard doesn't suit you at all. You should shave it off. Goodbye.'

What me? Evil? Lustful? Well, maybe. What was wrong with lust, anyway? And who was I in bondage to? Lord Of Material Success! Lord Of The Gates Of Matter! What balderdash! Arrant nonsense! Just wait until I tell Holmes about this. He'll laugh his bloody head off.

I had forgotten about the nasty business at hand. When I stepped out of the caravan and adjusted to the blinding sunlight, my emotions began to calm down slowly and I remembered what we were investigating and why we were there.

Macaroni and his people were sitting around, smoking and chatting. Lestrade strode up the field, followed by a dozen bobbies. There was no sign of Holmes. I hoped he hadn't vanished on another of his jaunts without telling anyone. He was getting a little too old for that game. Actually, the Reichenbach Falls had been more than enough for me. Three years! And not a word!

Lestrade and I spent the following few tedious hours in the fruitless exercise of interviewing each of the carnival workers, none of whom knew anything about dead babies, with or without heads. Surprise, surprise. But they were a rough-looking, shifty-eyed lot, whom I suspected were expert at straddling the thin line between legal and illegal activities. Not for a minute did I trust their heavy silences and pretended ignorance. It would not have surprised me if several of them had seen the inside of Pentonville Prison, including Tony Macaroni himself. Most of these men were related to the carnival owner in some way or another, so it was all very much a family affair.

At my query, the impatient dwarf explained to us that Isabelle Chilikov, or Madame Oracle, had been picked up on the side of a mountainous forest road in Bulgaria a few months earlier, hungry, pregnant and in need of help, as the so-called father, a local priest, had refused to accept any paternity in the case. Her hirsute appearance was the result of a hormonal imbalance and she earned her keep by reading cards and appearing on stage as 'The Bearded Lady'.

The afternoon wore on and still no Holmes. Where on earth had he got to? Lestrade's men had found nothing of value on the site, so the young detective was forced to accede to the growing demands of Tony Macaroni that the carnival be allowed to finish packing up and leave, in time to catch the late ferry to France. I tried to persuade him to find some legal reason to detain the crew of roustabouts, but failed. Jasper Lestrade insisted on doing everything by the book and following 'procedure', not wanting to damage his future career by disobeying orders. Having decided to ignore Holmes' advice and place a 'missing girl' advertisement in the next day's papers, he returned with his men to searching the heath for the baby's head.

Feeling disappointed with the lack of initiative shown by young Lestrade, and worried about my dear old companion, I left Hampstead for 221B Baker Street in the early evening by growler. I was exhausted and my throbbing leg insisted on recalling those distant traumatic years in the Afghan desert. Nevertheless I did manage a short nap on the way home, something that my body had grown used to in my declining years.

This helped to set me up for an overexcited Lily Hudson, who wanted to know every single thing that had happened, down to the 'smowles' de'ayl'. As she had prepared a sumptuous cold plate of chicken, ham, beetroot salad and my favourite red Leicester cheese, I acquiesced. If I remember correctly, the Lord opened his Gates Of Matter by gobbling Holmes' entire share of the food that evening, having had little or no lunch.

With Lily back in her 'slave quawters', as she called them, after a pipe or two of fresh birdseye and a hefty brandy, my irritation at the continued absence of Holmes grew into anxiety. What if he had been attacked and kidnapped? Or, heaven forbid, murdered? In the same year that we had joined forces again after almost two decades apart? Where was the justice in that?

But in my heart of hearts I knew that justice had little place in our lives upon this troubled planet, and so I spent another restless night, dozing on and off and dreaming this time of being chased around the Tunnel Of Love by a muscular bearded Amazonian woman with an axe in the shape of a giant Tarot card. It was a relief to finally wake up. I vowed never to eat cheese late at night again.

As August passed into September and October and the trees in Regent Park finally lost their yellow leaves, there was still no news of Holmes, and no progress either by Lestrade on the headless baby case. The head had not been found and no parent had come forward to claim the unfortunate child as their own. The inquest produced no new information, and the corpse was duly interred in an unnamed pauper's grave in Whitechapel. Interest in the subject began to wane, although the disappearance of the world's first consulting detective had been discovered by an inquisitive freelance reporter, who overheard Lily and Jasper chatting about him in a local tea-shop. Disrespectful headlines such as 'Sherlock Holmes Vanishes Yet Again. Bye, Bye.' and 'Return To The Reichenbach Falls?' appeared in the gutter press. An old daguerrotype of Holmes, hopelessly out of date, was accompanied by the caption: 'Have You Seen This Sleuth?' I certainly would not have recognised him. There was even an untimely obituary published in the Daily Telegraph, which necessitated a sternly-worded letter from yours truly, threatening the full weight of the law unless it was retracted.

By mid-November, I was beginning to accept the awful possibility that the bell may have finally tolled for the great detective. What would I do then? Return to the loneliness of Paddington?

But one blustery Thursday a telegram arrived for me, which raised my hopes, although I could make neither head nor tail of it. I had to assume that it was some sort of coded message from Holmes. I asked Lily to sit down with me and try to decipher its contents, as she had

certain skills in that area. Yet all the telegram contained was a set of 6*6 numbers:
314159-265358-979323-846264-338314-111111.

Lily assumed immediately that it was some sort of book code, with page numbers, followed by line numbers, followed by positions within line. Without knowing the book, such a code is impossible to break. We tried the Bible, but only a string of rubbish transpired.

After a few hours of fruitless endeavour with Bradshaw, Whitaker's Almanac and several popular works of literature, I became frustrated and gave up, retiring to my pipe by the crackling fire. My head was buzzing with these meaningless numbers. What had Holmes got against the English language? Why did everything have to be a puzzle with him? Why couldn't he use the telephone, like everybody else? What was he trying to tell us? Where in blazes was he?

But Lily would not give up. She was like a terrier worrying an old bone. Even when she had to go downstairs to cook my lunch, she took the telegram with her.

After a relaxing pipe of Arcadia ship's tobacco, I had just begun to doze off gently when I heard a shriek from the kitchen, followed by the thump, thump, thump of her clodhoppers on the wooden stairs.

'Oi fink oi've go' summa', deary.'

She sat down on the wicker chair beside me.

'See this foist foive sets o' numbairs? If oi puts a do' aftair the foist numbair, an' connects 'em, wot oi gets is the numbair 3.14159265358979323846264338314.'

'But that's Pi, isn't it?' I said. 'In mathematics, it's the ratio of the circumference of a circle to its diameter. It is an irrational number that goes on forever without a pattern of any kind. And it is one of the basic building blocks of our universe.'

'Wotevair. Oi go' it in moi li''le puzz'l buke. Oi fink Mr. 'Olmes dahn't mean nah numbair. Oi fink Mr. 'Olmes, he mean the le''ers P an' I. Put 'em with the le''ers O,N,E,S from the raist, an' we gets P-I-O-N-E-S.'

'Ponies!' I shouted.

'Yeah, maiybe,' said Lily. 'Smawl hawrses.'

Ponies. This was too much of a coincidence. Was Holmes telling me that ponies were responsible for the child's death on the heath? Or was he saying something else?

'It awlsow mean caish, dunnit? Twenny-foive quids, oi fink.'

'What, Lily? Oh, yes, a pony is considered to equate to twenty-five pounds, in slang terms. But I don't think that's relevant here. These ponies would be of the small horse variety. The telegram must have something to do with the headless baby case.'

'An' in moi coickknee slaing, it equaytes tah a macarowni.'

'Yes. Yes, of course. Wait a minute, Lily. What did you say?'

'The coickknee slaing fer a caish powny is a macarowni.'

'The cockney slang for a cash pony is a macaroni.' I had to repeat the sentence out loud to believe what I had just heard. Macaroni. Macaroni's Carnival. If I had been able to, I would surely have leapt from my chair in excitement. As it was, I merely stood up stiffly and shook her hand to congratulate her.

'That's it, Lily! You are a genius! Holmes is telling us to find the Macaroni Carnival, wherever it is running at the moment. Get Lestrade on the phone and ask him to trace the movements of this funfair after it left London. No, no, wait. I'll do it. Splendid work! Good girl!'

It transpired that the carnival had travelled from France through Switzerland, Italy, Yugoslavia and thence to Bulgaria, before returning to Belgium via Romania, Hungary, Austria and Germany. Its current location was a small seaside resort on the Flemish Coast in West Flanders called Koksijde. Having explained the message from Holmes and its possible implications to Jasper Lestrade, I persuaded him to join me on the next available ferry to Ostend. From there we took a tram along the coast to Koksijde, arriving in the early evening.

'Pretty little place,' said Lestrade, as we alighted.

'Windy little place,' I replied, buttoning my coat against the strong breeze.

'I need to get some assistance from my associates at the local cop shop, just in case there's any ruckus later on. Then we'll follow you down to the carnival. Let's hope something comes out of all this, and that we can locate Mr. Holmes. Will you be okay on your own, Doctor?'

This question from a mere child to Sherlock Holmes' lifelong assistant did not merit a reply, so I gave Lily's boyfriend my most withering gaze and turned towards the sprawling beach, where distant lights and music heralded a display of some sort. I had packed my old Webley Service revolver inside my coat, and fingered it comfortingly as I strode along the bustling waterfront like any normal tourist, but with a hat pulled down over my head and scarf around my face in case a carnival worker remembered me from the earlier interviews.

I recognised the pleasure-wheel first. Despite the wind, it was circling at considerable speed, to a chorus of screams of pure fear from people stupid enough to derive fun from putting their lives at risk. Then the others – the roller-coaster, bumper cars, carousel, galloper, high striker etc., etc., This time there were many more of the brilliantly coloured vardoes. They were all marked with the same name: Macaroni's Carnival. It was the fairground of the ponies.

I had formed no clear plan to find Holmes, so I wandered between some hilly tussocks of wiry marram grass close to the tents and lurid sideshows, keeping a keen eye open for the mottled dwarf or the bearded lady. Sure enough, I discovered her live show at the edge of a huge sand dune, near a shallow pool of glinting sea-water. A queue of noisy youngsters were lined up in front. She had clearly not taken my advice about shaving. A beardless fat roustabout was urging other customers to enter her domain.

'Roll up, roll up. Come see the bearded lady!'

I passed on swiftly through some furze and scrub, having no wish to meet that appalling fortune-teller ever again in this life. Turning a corner I passed a villainous-looking gypsy twirling a hurdy-gurdy. He was obviously responsible for the music. This was followed by a coconut shy, a pained looking sword-swallower, and an enormous strongman, busily bending a steel rod into the shape of a V in front of some admiring children.

Then I noticed a large fluttering tent with a handwritten sign outside, which said '*Freaks – All types of human oddities – entrance only one frank*'. Normally I would avoid such a disgraceful show like the plague, but for a reason that could only be explained as a feeling in my waters, I decided to pay over my money to a roustie, keep my head down, face covered and pass between the flaps.

A clear track had been stamped into the tawny sand, with metal cages to the right for the curious to peep into. A couple of young girls ahead of me giggled their way past the exhibits. I can tell you now that I have witnessed many damaged figures in Afghanistan, mainly the result of jezail bullet wounds to the face, but I have never seen such an array of human deformities as were on display here. There was the customary pair of female siamese twins conjoined at the waist, a two-headed man with webbed feet, a woman with a growth on her stomach that was so large that she looked like a mushroom, a four-legged boy, a hairy wolf-man, a child with scales on his face like a fish, another young boy with two noses where his eyes should have been and finally an old man who looked strangely like Joseph Merrick, the famous elephant man, to my saddened eyes. His head was malformed, his spine was curved, he had the same lumpy skin and an overgrown right arm and hand. All these creatures were shackled in irons to the floor. It really should be banned, this wanton commercial exploitation of the less fortunate!

The elephant man was gurning, rocking back and forth on his knees, arms folded within a straitjacket around his body. His single eye glared at me from his gargoyled features. I shook my head in despair at the destiny of some, and had pushed the exit flap back, when I heard a faint whisper of the following immortal words.

'So you decoded my telegram?'

I froze in shock, gripping the flap for support. My gammy leg started an agitated twitch. It was the voice of Holmes. I would recognise it at any pitch.

'Your disguise is adequate to dupe the rousties, but you will have to work a little harder to fool me, Watson.'

No, I was not dreaming. I needed to turn around and find the source of the murmuring voice that I knew as well as my own.

'You must admit that my camouflage is better than yours.'

The words were coming from the elephant man! Yet his demeanour was still the same as before, although he had stopped rocking back and forth and his eye no longer glared at me.

'Holmes,' I breathed in disbelief. 'Is it really you? What happened? Why are you like this?'

The muttering voice rose a decibel in urgency.

'Time enough for explanations later. You must contact the Belgian police and inform them that Sherlock Holmes has been kidnapped, having uncovered a network of child trafficking within Europe, behind the camouflage of a fairground carnival. Organised by Tony Macaroni, and with the explicit involvement of every member of his Roma tribe.'

Holmes paused. His voice broke when he continued.

'The headless baby was an innocent by-product of this horrendous crime. I will tell everyone the full story back in 221B Baker Street, if you can get me there. For the time being, I am somewhat indisposed in this damned elephant suit. Hurry, Watson! Someone is coming!'

A single customer had entered the tent. When I looked around at Holmes again, he had resumed his rocking to and fro and the single eye glared out at me again. Reluctant as I was to leave my dear old friend chained up like this, we old soldiers are familiar with the chain of command and so I knew exactly what I had to do.

Three evenings later we were sitting around a blazing log fire in 221B Baker Street, waiting for a somewhat revived Holmes to explain everything to myself, Lily and Jasper. He had slept all the way back to England, and for another two days afterwards, having been released by me from his freakish captivity in the elephant man suit of armour. Now the great detective, clad in his familiar mousy dressing-gown, was fiddling with his pipe, which kept going out. I noticed that Lily and Jasper were holding hands in anticipation of the full story.

This loyal soldier had obeyed his orders. He had assisted Lestrade and the combined Koksijde and Ostend police force to round up the crew. Some of them had vanished into the Belgian night, never to be seen again, but the main players were captured and in prison, awaiting trial for kidnapping, with further charges to come. Including the miniscule Tony Macaroni, that demon of demons. Evidence of their crimes was to be found inside the vardoes.

'While I was examining the corpse of that little girl in Hampstead Heath ...', began Holmes, when he had finally fixed his pipe and was puffing away towards the ceiling. 'I noticed immediately that the arterial connections from the neck to her head were not normal. My first thought, which is usually the right one, was that she had been killed for exactly that reason. My second thought was an even uglier one. That she had been killed because she was worthless, in the true sense of the word. Having been solving crimes for a period of almost fifty years, I believe this to have been the most difficult case of my career. I have never known such a filthy evil. Evil in its purest form. Bear with me, Watson.'

'Of course. But I ... *we* would just like to know why you did not communicate with us any sooner, or even right from the beginning,' I interrupted. With some asperity, I admit. And actually I would have liked to join him as a roustie, although I might not have made a very good one. It sounded like fun.

'I intended to, old fellow, do believe me. Events rather ran away from me. To continue. The red string was an obvious connection to the Macaroni Romas, but I needed to find out what was behind the killing of that child. After a few minutes of examining the galloper ponies that day in August, I realised the magnitude of the job facing us. A different approach was undoubtedly needed. Then I remembered that I had hidden a disguise in a niche to the rear of a Flask Walk gate lodge many years earlier, as was my practice back then. It was still there, although a little the worse for wear, and not exactly roustabout gear, but good enough for me to pass myself off as an experienced grey-bearded carnival worker, desperately looking for a job.'

'When I finally returned to the site in Pryors Field, you pair were busy interviewing the crew. They needed an extra hand and I was welcomed by Tony Macaroni himself, who invited me to join the carnival on its journey across Europe, on condition that I would never leave the campsite, not even for one hour. It was not an ideal arrangement, but I agreed. I was even able to practice a little of my limited Romany on Lestrade when he got around to interrogating me: *"Me mangav te jav ando granitza tumensa."* In other words, *"I want to go to the border with you."* '

'That was you in that awful shaggy beard?' muttered Lestrade. 'Good grief!'

'One of your better camouflages, Holmes,' I added. But he was immune to my irony.

'Thank you, Watson. It was a good test of my disguise. I figured that if you two did not see through it, then I could safely carry it off with my carnival co-workers.'

Holmes drew on his pipe contentedly.

'I travelled with the crew to Bulgaria, via France, Switzerland, Italy and Yugoslavia, spending about ten days in each country. I felt that I was being watched all the time, but the other workers came gradually to trust the old hand. Although he could undertake no heavy work, he was always ready to help and seemed to know what to do in many situations. Have I never confessed to you, Watson, my teenage desire to run away from home and join a circus?'

'No. I must have missed that,' I sighed. I was beginning to realise that Holmes was simply incapable of considering the feelings of other people when he was involved in a case. We are what we are.

'Yes. For the first few weeks everything went quite well, despite my lack of Royal Jelly, which is not easily available when travelling on the road. I began to notice some oddities about the way the carnival operated. For instance, there were no children about, and I saw only one woman. We had been joined in Paris by another set of vans which had travelled ahead. Each of these was kept under strict lock and key at all times, including every night. And all the windows had been painted black on the inside. So I had few opportunites for exploration. The takings were handed over to the diminutive manager himself, who wandered around every evening like a postman, with a canvas bag over his shoulder, collecting the money from the shows and rides.'

'I carried out my daily tasks and kept an eye open for evidence of any suspicious activity involving children. I found none until the end of September, after our arrival in Bulgaria at the site of their permanent base. By that time I had become quite friendly with Giuseppe Macaroni, one of Toni's five brothers. He was the strongman act, who used to keep us awake at night when he had indulged himself too much at the local inn, by slamming a fifteen-pound sledge-hammer onto the high striker, ringing the bell loudly again and again. I had also been introduced to Madame Oracle, one Isabelle Chilikov, the 'Bearded Lady', who was pregnant at the time.'

I snorted involuntarily.

Holmes smiled indulgently. 'I see that you may also have met her, Watson. Did she tell your future by the Tarots, and was it upsetting?'

'Yes,' I bridled. 'A bit. Apparently I am an evil, greedy, lustful trickster. And a liar to boot.'

I ignored the efforts being made by Lestrade and Lily to suppress their smiles.

'Really?' replied Holmes. 'If it is any consolation to you, my dear fellow, she also predicted that I would die an extremely violent death within five years at the foot of a huge waterfall. I suspect that she may have been reading some of your earlier tales. But she claimed that the cards never lied.'

Holmes paused, narrowed his eyes and stared into space, as though struggling to recall the sequence of events.

'One day we were preparing to leave the site in Bulgaria. I was passing by Isabelle's exotic vardoe when Toni Macaroni vaulted down from her stoop, carrying a small bundle in his hands. He was followed by a volley of screams and abuse in a language that I recognised vaguely as Bulgarian. He was in such a hurry that he forgot to lock the door. As soon as the pigmy was out of sight, I grabbed my opportunity and climbed into the van, only to find a weeping Isabelle, kicking her legs up and down in frustration. Legs that had been chained to the floor.'

' "Hamish," she cried. Eh, my chosen name was Hamish Watson. I do hope you don't mind, Doctor?'

'Oh, any time, my dear chap. Be my guest,' I replied.

' "Hamish, he take my little baby away. My little Ivana gone forever, he say. He give me just seventy lev and then he lock me up, like this. I pregnant again, too. One of his brothers ..." Her voice tailed off into a howling of sheer misery.'

'I felt that I was getting my first insight into the dreadful business that lay hidden behind the bright lights of the carnival. And nearing a solution to the case of the headless baby at the same time. I needed to see what was inside the other vardoes, to confirm my theory, even if it meant my disguise being discovered. I tried to calm Isabelle down by promising that I would free her from captivity when I had the evidence I needed. She and the others are all as innocent in this affair as any one of us, Lestrade. I hope that you will remember this.'

'I most certainly will,' said Lestrade promptly.

'But she was still doing her show a few days ago,' I declared.

'Under some form of control, I'm sure, Watson. What else could she do until she was freed? She may have hoped to get her child back at some stage.'

'But she must have known what was going on,' I persisted. 'She wasn't shackled when she read my damned future.'

'No. At that stage she was still the helpless refugee, rescued by the Macaronis,' continued Holmes. 'To get back to the story. I decided to throw caution to the wind, wait for the dwarf to return and waylay him for the keys, then open the vans and take the consequences. I explained my desperate plan to Isabelle and she offered me a scarf to tie him up with. Then I hid behind a curtain that fronted a makeshift toilet. In a couple of minutes I heard him returning up the stoop. I waited until he had passed the toilet, then grabbed him from behind, lifted him into the air and banged his head firmly off the roof. He was too dazed to put up a fight as I wound the scarf around his body several times, trussing him up like a Christmas turkey. He could neither move nor speak when I had finished. I unhooked his keys from his belt and dashed out of the vardoe.'

Holmes tamped his pipe down thoughtfully with his finger.

'The first one that I opened was empty. But the remaining ten all contained the same scene. Exactly what I had expected to find.'

Holmes halted abruptly. For effect, I thought.

'What was it?' the three of us chorussed impatiently.

'Each of the remaining vans held a single woman at a different stage of gestation. Doped and chained to the floor. One was close to giving birth and was moaning away like a beached seal.'

'Holmes!' I exclaimed. 'What a description!'

'Eh, my apologies, Watson, old chap. Of course, you have seen that sort of thing many times, but I have not.

Anyway my suspicions had been confirmed. These women were being systematically impregnated against their will. Time and time again. Subsequently, after my disguise had been discovered and I had been captured, Tony Macaroni was only too happy to explain the entire business. Presumably he imagined that I was not going to live to tell the tale to anyone. These vagabond women were picked up along the carnival route and seduced with offers of performing on stage. Each regular roustabout – they were all in on it, of course, the whole Macaroni family – took turns to be responsible for a girl, raping her until she became pregnant, and then looking after her during her term. Any objections were met with injections of laudanum. When the children had been born and nurtured for a period of time, they were taken away from their mothers, who would already be pregnant again by then.'

'What happened to the little ones?' I asked, scarcely able to believe my ears.

'They were sold. Macaroni had a list of clients spread all over Europe, including England, where middle-class parents are apparently prepared to pay up to five thousand pounds for a baby.'

'Five thousand!' Lestrade whistled in astonishment.

'Yes. This filthy business was hugely profitable to the Macaroni family, and the carnival provided the perfect cover. They could travel wherever they wanted. If they heard of a customer in Spain, they could head down there.'

'Can't we trace the children and give them back to their natural mothers?' I queried.

'I very much doubt whether it is worth it,' replied Holmes. 'Presumably they are treasured by their wealthy surrogate parents, and have much better lives. I think I'll leave that problem to you, Lestrade.'

'Oh, thank you,' said the Scotland Yard detective drily.

'Those poor women,' I muttered.

'When was yer fahnd aht?' asked Lily.

'Fairly quickly. It had not escaped the attention of the rousties that I was exposing their crimes to the world. I was accosted immediately after the last van was opened. They stood around me in a circle. I whipped off my beard and told them who I was and that they were all under arrest. They laughed, and closed in on me. Giusseppe placed his massive arms around me and carried me over to the high-striker, where he strung me up at the back by my jacket. I hung there until they had released Tony Macaroni. The fuming dwarf decided that my punishment lay inside the freak's tent, wrapped in a straitjacket and moulded into the elephant man's shape with a solution of plaster of Paris. All the exhibits were forced to perform in the freak show, on pain of starvation and beatings. And we were being watched most of the time. I imagine that I was destined for a watery end on the trip across to England.'

'You were like that for almost six weeks?' Lestrade queried.

'My dear chap.' It was all I could bring myself to say. And me complaining about his lack of contact over the period. My heart sank with shame.

'Yes. It was quite an interesting experience, being in harness for a considerable length of time, without much movement, apart from the obvious compulsory breaks. The mind takes over. I contemplated many different subjects in considerable depth, consciously recalling my research from my cerebral cortex. Captivity also provided

45

me with an opportunity to relive every single case of my previous life. I passed the time by assessing when, or if, I had made a mistake in any of my deductions. There were surprisingly few. "The Adventure Of The Yellow Face" stands out.'

'Norbery!' I had not forgotten.

'Exactly. Actually it felt more like six months. I was affectively bound and gagged until my Boswell rescued me the other day, in response to my telegram.'

'But 'ow did yer get the bleedin' telligraim aht?' demanded Lily.

'And how was the baby decapitated?' asked Lestrade. 'Where is the head?'

'And were other unwanted babies killed in the same way?' I ventured.

'One at a time, please. First, the headless baby. I don't know, Watson, if other babies have suffered the loss of their life in the same way. It is possible, as this business has been going on for over ten years. That benighted pseudo-Irish cockney midget boasted about it. I don't suppose I could have ten minutes alone with him some time, could I, Lestrade? Just me and my life preserver?'

'It's out of my hands, Mr. Holmes. The Belgians have first option on that. And there are other countries that are interested in solving certain missing women cases. But justice will be served on all of the Macaronis. You may take my word on it.'

'Hhmm. Giusseppe Macaroni, my so-called strongman friend would visit me occasionally in the freak's tent, often late at night, to avoid detection by his relatives. I believe he felt bad about his role in my capture. One night, after he had sampled a firkin of ale somewhere, he confessed to me that it was he who had placed the unfortunate paralysed infant face down upon the steel base of the high striker and used his sledge-hammer to the effect of knocking off her block. He had been ordered to do so by his brother, of course, who saw no financial value in a paralysed baby, and wanted no risk of it ... *she*, being identified. Apparently her name was Amelia. Tony took the head, and Giusseppe hid the remainder where it was found.'

'Great God Almighty,' I muttered. 'Such savagery. The man should be hung, drawn and quartered.' A sledge-hammer!

'His guilt at this horrendous crime was considerable, but he redeemed himself somewhat by sending that telegram to you. Mind you, I did convince him that the sequence of numbers was merely a string of bets on the Kempton Park races. He believed me. A simple soul, Giusseppe. It is a pity ...'

'Don't worry, Mr. Holmes. I'll see that the court has all of the facts at their disposal. But I doubt if he will avoid the full weight of the law.' Lestrade was beginning to glance at his watch. 'I think I may have to go now. Reports to write, etc.,'

'Very well. Lily will see you out. Thank you again for your help, young Lestrade. You'll go far.'

Once the lovey-dovey pair had descended the stairs, I scraped out my pipe and refilled it.

'Why the coded telegram, Holmes?' I asked. 'Why not spell your situation out in words of the English language?

'I was concerned that Guisseppe might show it to his brother. And I knew that you and Lily, with your brains and her knowledge of cockney rhyming slang, would crack it fairly quickly together.'

'It was mostly Lily's doing.' Nevertheless, his flattery was appreciated. 'And so poor little Amelia's head has never been found?' I continued, drawing sadly on my fresh pipe.

'Apparently not,' replied Holmes.

'But where can it be?'

'Tony Macaroni probably hid it beneath another set of branches, or buried it in an entirely different part of the heath, to avoid identification,' said Holmes. 'It awaits discovery by another precious child one day, whose dreams will surely be enlivened then. Oh, yes! Hah! Oh! Hee, hee! What a thought! Hoh, hoh! I'd like to be there! Hee!'

'Really, Holmes. You have such a twisted sense of humour. I can see nothing remotely amusing about this case, and am just pleased that it is over and done with, and a number of innocent women and children can be protected from this disgusting trafficking. And that you are safe and well, of course.'

'Oh, so am I, old fellow. So am I. A society that does not protect its children is not a society worth preserving. Indeed. But at least our friend Tony Macaroni will sample the pleasures of capital punishment before too long. A short rope should do it. I'd like to be there for that, too. They'll need a much longer and stronger one for Giusseppe, though.'

Holmes yawned. 'I can tell you, Watson, that the life of a roustabout is not all tea and buns. Heaving and shoving that equipment around has left my body in need of sustenance. Who'd be a gypsy, eh? Well, goodnight, old fellow.'

Sherlock Holmes rose from his chair abruptly and entered his bedroom, closing the door firmly behind him.

I knocked out my pipe and followed suit shortly afterwards, wondering if I had said something to upset him.

It was not until the next morning, after he had failed to appear for breakfast, and an alarmed Lily discovered him sprawled upon the floor of his room, still fully clothed, breathing stentoriously, the bloody cocaine needle dripping from his left forearm, that the full impact of this foul case upon the mind, heart and soul of the world's first consulting detective became only too shockingly apparent.

3.   Sherlock Holmes And The Chelsea Necrophile.

'Well, Watson,' said Holmes, flicking over the pages of his Times newspaper. 'What about it? Do you believe that we living organisms can communicate with the dead?'

'Great Scott, Holmes!' I protested, through a mouthful of toast. 'What a question at breakfast!'

It was Christmas Eve in the year of our Lord 1925, and Holmes was still recovering from his nightmare as a captive freak at Macaroni's Carnival. The case of the headless baby had so unnerved him that he had returned to his daily seven-per-cent solution of cocaine, after an initial overdose that almost did for him. I knew that loss of appetite and sleeplessness were side-effects of the drug, and I noticed the great detective had not touched Lily's excellent eggs and bacon. Yet I could not find it in my heart to criticise him. I am uncertain as to my own reaction to being covered in plaster-of-paris and held in a straitjacket for almost six weeks, masquerading as the elephant man. I imagine that I would go insane without my daily toilet.

'There is a case here,' continued Holmes, as though I had not opened my mouth, 'describing a woman in Peru who kept her dead husband beside her in bed for a period of almost three years. She embalmed him, dressed him in his pyjamas and put him to bed, and has been behaving as though he were still alive all that time. She claimed that he smelled exactly the same and talked back to her. They argued as they had always done. No table-rapping or séances, just Spanish. She has been placed in an asylum.'

I pushed my unfinished meal away from me in disgust.

'Thank you, Holmes, for destroying my appetite,' I said coldly. 'And if you must know, I do believe that *some* form of communication is possible between the living and the dead. If a person believes in the afterlife, as I do, why should it not be possible to contact the souls that frequent it?'

Holmes put down his newspaper and looked at me with what I assumed to be genuine interest.

'Have you ever tried to talk to either of your wives? Using spiritualism?' he asked.

'Yes, actually. I have.'

'And ...?'

'I attended a séance shortly after Bea passed away,' I sighed, knowing full well what Holmes would think of such diversions. 'I was a bit depressed at the time. It was one of those ouija board affairs.'

'What happened?'

'Nothing. Absolute silence. No movement of the planchette at all. There were several other people in attendance, and each one managed some form of response. But not me. I just wanted to make sure she was happy in summerland,' I added defensively.

'Summerland?' queried Holmes.

'It is what spiritualists call heaven.'

'My dear chap, you must be extremely susceptible to the power of suggestion. You do realise that all previous examples of paranormal activities have proven to be pure chicanery, don't you? And that most mediums have been discovered to be frauds, who prey on the grief of the recently bereaved? The Fox sisters in Hydesville, New York, with their mysterious table-rappings, later confessed to having caused them by cracking their toe and ankle joints underneath their skirts. The Davenport

Brothers, who tied themselves up in a so-called 'spirit cabinet' containing musical instruments and pretended that music was being played from inside, were found to be the humbug brothers when a pair of amateur magicians used a knot that wasn't so easy to remove. There are many more such examples. Your good wife was silent because she simply was not present. I would lay a bet that you were asked to hold hands so as not to disrupt the trickery, and that you were probably in the dark, to heighten your sensitivity to sound and movement, make it all a bit scarey and to camouflage the actions of the medium.'

Holmes folded up his newspaper and propped it against the teapot as he resumed his mild harangue earnestly.

'Believe me, I spent many a long hour trussed up in that damned freak tent, thinking about this very subject as I anticipated my own watery demise. The logical conclusion I reached is that all forms of spiritual belief are a mere disguise for a preoccupation with death, and the idea of dying. There is no supernatural, Watson, only the natural, all of which will some day be explained by science. Fairies do not frolic at the bottom of the garden, but in fake photographs of cardboard cutouts, like that Cottingley lot. Alas, I fear that Charles Darwin is correct with his theory of evolution. We are naught but intelligent apes, and when we die, that is the end of everything. It is exactly the same for us as it was for the last insect that you stood upon by accident. Except that we make a bigger fuss about it.'

'But I cannot believe that this short life span is all there is, Holmes. There must be something else,' I insisted, pouring coffee for myself. 'Don't you believe in the existence of a higher power or Supreme Being?'

'As I have told you before, no. I do not,' replied Holmes firmly. 'That particular construct only began about thirty thousand years ago, when the human brain became large enough to encompass the idea of creationism, and to yearn for some form of personal immortality. Hence the notion of the soul and life after death, which would not have been countenanced by earlier primates, because their brains were too small. They were too stupid, if you like. I have been delving into 'On The Origin Of Species by Means of Natural Selection' since my return from incarceration. You should read it. It might broaden your mind.'

'I have already done so. I do not believe his findings. Who made the apes we are supposed to be descended from? And my mind is broad enough, thank you,' I stated flatly.

'Basically the apes evolved from reptiles, who evolved from fish. Over hundreds of millions of years, of course.'

'Fish?' I cried. 'Do you mean that this poor fellow is a distant relative of yours? A fourth cousin many times removed, perhaps?'

I held up a smoked kipper with a broad smile on my face. To me, Darwin's theory seemed quite as farfetched as that of a benevolent God.

'Oh well, if you're going to be pawky about it,' said Holmes blithely, standing up. 'I suppose we shall both discover the lie about life after death soon enough. If I go first, perhaps you can try to contact me through a medium, and I ... maybe I will do the same for you, if vice versa. Agreed?'

'If you like,' I replied, feeling that I had scored a definite point. 'Would you like some coffee?'

'No, thank you. I'm for my morning pipe.'

Holmes headed for the mantlepiece and his dried plugs and dottles from the previous day.

At the time of this cheerful conversation I did not realise that it would form a beguiling prelude to one of our oddest investigations, which would serve to highlight our separate beliefs about the afterlife.

As we were both in our seventies now and had just completed a difficult case, a long period of recuperation was on the cards. I was looking forward to a relaxing Christmas, with plenty of home cooking and a tot or two of cherry brandy. I hoped that Holmes would not be too morose when the heightening effect of his drug wore off, and he could enjoy the Yuletide with me. But consulting detectives cannot always choose the timing of their problems, as the slam of a carriage door, followed by the chiming of the doorbell at 221B Baker Street, testified.

'I wonder who that could be on such a filthy day?' mused Holmes, fiddling a pipe cleaner through his churchwarden clay.

'We shall soon see,' I suggested, as Lily's clodhoppers thumped their way up the stairs.

'Rev'rent Tomays fer Mr. 'Olmes,' announced Lily Hudson, our cheerful cockney housekeeper and niece of the late Martha Hudson.

Lily stepped to one side and her curvaceous figure was replaced in our view by a bent ascetic-looking clergyman with piercing blue eyes sunk deeply into somewhat crumpled features, who kept fidgeting with his collar as though it were too tight around his neck. His cloak sparkled with drops of rain and his shoes squelched slightly as he entered the room with a stiffened gait, removing a wide-brimmed floppy hat. He reminded me of our old nemesis, the late, unlamented Professor Moriarty, whose body had never actually been recovered after his fall into the Reichenbach stream in the Bernese Oberland region of Switzerland all those years ago.

'Reverend,' said Holmes, relinquishing his pipe-work and shaking hands warmly with the cleric. 'So good of you to drop in on us. May I introduce my friend and colleague, Dr. John Watson? You may remember, Watson, that Canon Thomas was kind enough to allow me to conduct the funeral service for my brother Mycroft at the Chelsea All Saints, albeit somewhat disguised. Here. Let me take your coat. Do sit down by the fire and warm yourself.'

'Dr. Watson. A pleasure to meet you. Thank you, Mr. Holmes. It is bitter cold out there,' said the clergyman in a high-pitched, faintly Irish brogue, yielding his topcoat and hat. He eased himself onto the basket-chair with evident relief, his twin shocks of white hair bouncing gently about his ears.

'Happy Christmas, Canon Thomas,' I said. 'Have you had breakfast?'

'Yes, yes, yes. Please don't bother on my account. And do call me Adam.'

'Perhaps a cup of coffee?'

'No, no. I never touch caffeine. Eh, I have a rather puzzling tale to tell and am hoping that Mr. Holmes can shed some light upon it.'

We took the opportunity to light our pipes and seat ourselves comfortably in chairs facing the agitated cleric.

'I look forward to hearing it. Pray proceed. If I can be of assistance ...?' said Holmes, clearly engaged by the possibility of a fresh case. 'I perceive that you are a widower, have recently retired, deeply regret doing so, suffer from periodic attacks of gout as well as lateral epicondylitis in your left elbow, have moved out of Chelsea, and find your replacement cleric rather inadequate for the illustrious position you vacated.'

'But ...? How on earth did you kn..?' Reverend Thomas' eyebrows shot up, his face adopted the colour of chalk and his eyes were wide with fear, as though he had met his Maker.

'Forgive me my little games,' interrupted Holmes. 'Watson is quite used to them, and I sometimes forget that others are not. You have removed your wedding ring, which might be due to the death of your wife, or her departure to grasses greener. I suspect the former is most likely. It is plain that you have retired, judging by your layman's dress. Your presence and the hat give you away. On Christmas Eve a working Canon would certainly be busy in church. You informed me in February earlier this year that you hoped never to retire. Walking carefully without using either of your big toes is a sure sign of too much uric acid in the blood, or arthritic gout. You keep fingering your left elbow, a common occurrence with sufferers of that painful condition, tennis elbow. I assumed that a retired cleric would no longer be allowed to live in the vicarage, and forgive me, but that Chelsea would prove beyond your means. Now, please. Do tell your story.'

'Well, yes, my wife passed away several months ago. I was forced to retire and move to Wimbledon. I don't know why. I've only just turned eighty. Eh, what about my inadequate replacement?' squeaked Canon Thomas, his face returning to its customary greyish hue.

'Reverend, how could anybody possibly match those masterful sermons on the nature of sin, your stirring preachings on hell, fire and damnation, that deep knowledge of the Scriptures and other sacred texts, combined, of course, with your sensitivity to the moral and social needs of your parish? It would be impossible, I feel.'

The reedy cleric squirmed at Holmes' rather unctuous complements.

'Eh, thank you, Mr. Holmes. It is nice to know one is not forgotten. Now, my story. Where shall I begin?'

'I suggest that the beginning might be as good an answer to that question as any,' said Holmes, arching an eyebrow.

Reverend Thomas fingered his collar yet again, leaned forward and opened his hands tentatively to the roaring flames of the fire.

'Yes. Well. Ahem. I continue to be a faithful member of the Chelsea All-Saints parish, and attend Choral Evensong there every Sunday evening, as I did last weekend,' he said. 'I retain a position as a churchwarden and had some duties to attend to, after my replacement retired to the vicarage across the road for the night. I thought that I was alone in the church after collecting and storing the church hymnals, and I was about to close and lock the doors when I was startled by the thunderous sound of the pipe organ. It had begun to play Bach's Toccata and Fugue in D minor. Slightly tinnily, I might add. I assumed our organist, Mr. Algernon Birdwhistle, had remained behind to practice his playing. I listened critically as I returned to the stairs that led up to the pipes.'

Canon Thomas placed his head in his hands, and moaned, almost to himself, 'You cannot imagine what I found there.'

'Do tell,' whispered Holmes.

The distressed clergyman raised his head and looked wildly at the pair of us.

'Nothing! There was noone there! The keys were going up and down, exactly as though they were being played. As were the pedals. I thought maybe an apparition of some kind, a ghost even, was sitting on the stool, but I could neither see nor feel anything. Please do not consider that I was imagining any of this. Or that I suffer from delirium tremens or was under the influence of some powerful drug. And I am not insane.'

'Of course not, Canon,' I murmured sympathetically.

'But was the pipe organ not automated to play by itself sometimes? Like those available from the Aeolian Company? They are common enough, surely?' enquired Holmes.

'Oh, dear me, no. Indeed it is an original Bevington organ that has been there for over one hundred years. It needs replacing, if the truth be known.'

'What time was this?' asked Holmes.

'It would have been around 8.25pm,' replied the agitated vicar. 'But that is not the whole story. I left shortly afterwards and hurried home, badly rattled. I did not wish to inform my ... replacement, in case I really had imagined it! Then the next day I decided to return at the same time. And the same thing happened! In an empty church! And then again on Tuesday and Wednesday!'

'Was it always the same toccata, for the exact same length of time?' asked Holmes patiently.

'Yes. About two minutes. But yesterday I decided to take a closer look at the organ console. Astonishingly, a sequence of letters appeared before my eyes, spread across the thirty-two white keys on the bottom keyboard. They were clouded and shadowy, coming and going

58

continuously in time to the music, like a film out of focus. By concentrating my mind, I managed to write them down, hoping that they would tell me something before they disappeared when the music stopped. But I cannot fathom what that meaning is. Here.'

Canon Thomas handed a neatly folded piece of paper across to Holmes.

'I fear that God is trying to speak to me, and He is telling me that my time has come, Mr. Holmes,' Canon Thomas wailed.

'How do you know it isn't the other fellow?' murmured Holmes, without taking his eyes off the sheet of paper.

'Aarrgghh!' shrieked the clergyman.

'Holmes!' I protested.

He gave a start. 'Oh, forgive me, vicar. Just thinking aloud. This message is most diverting. Watson, the brandy.'

Canon Thomas recovered his self-control as he cupped his snifter in his hand and sipped gratefully. He peered hopefully above its rim at the great detective.

'Well? What do you make of it?' he asked.

'If it is God getting in touch with you, He certainly has a cryptic mind,' replied Holmes. 'The message might be some form of musical code, I suppose. He chose the right composer. Bach is full of such puzzles. How many keyboards does your Bevington possess?'

'Three,' replied Canon Thomas.

'May I?' I enquired.

'Of course.' Holmes handed me the paper.

While I perused the puzzle, Holmes continued his interview with the vicar.

'You have not informed your replacement yet about these events?' he queried.

'That is correct. He would assume a derangement of some kind. It would give the young whippersnapper too much pleasure to have me permanently detained in an asylum.'

Holmes sucked noisily on his pipe. 'Indeed. Does he have any whippersnappers of his own? Children, I mean?'

'Yes. Two young boys, aged fourteen and twelve. They ... they are not well-behaved. Horrible little monsters.'

'I see. And how many wardens does All-Saints have?'

'Three others. But they are away for the holidays. I must ring the bells myself.'

'Does anybody else work at the church, apart from the organist?'

'Only the ladies committee, who arrange the flowers and the polishing of pews and suchlike. They are headed by the vicar's wife, a formidable lady.'

'Do they all have keys of their own?'

'No. Only the vicar's wife. Sometimes I or one of my fellow wardens may have to let the ladies in, if she is away.'

Holmes' pipe sizzled, like a musical accompaniment to the workings of his brain.

'I need to confirm that you are absolutely convinced you were alone each time, inside the church?'

'Apart from whoever was playing that organ, yes.'

'Is there another service tonight?' asked Holmes.

'Oh, yes. There is always a children's pageant at six o'clock the evening before the anniversary of the birth of Our Saviour.'

Holmes stood up abruptly. 'Then we need keep you no longer, vicar. I suggest that we three meet this evening at the side entrance to the church. 8.10 sharp. Hopefully Watson and I can then experience the peculiar onanistic organ for ourselves, and do a bit more investigating into this little problem of yours. Be assured we shall occupy our time until then in attempting to break your ... message.'

After Lily had seen the vicar out into the teeming rain of Baker Street, I handed the note back to Holmes, having no notion whatsoever as to its meaning.

'It might equate to the music being played in some way,' I suggested weakly. 'Or it could be a form of automatic writing?'

'By the spirit of Johann Sebastian Bach? I doubt that, Watson. His authorship of this particular Toccata is still under question. Most sheet music was not signed in those distant days. But hopefully it will be a difficult nut to crack. Hah!' exclaimed Holmes, rubbing his hands together in glee. 'A supernatural question seeking a natural answer. A nice problem is the best Christmas present I could get. Did you know that Bach conceived some of his music in the form of crossword puzzles?'

'No. I did not.'

'Yes. He was a truly revolutionary composer,' Holmes continued enthusiastically. 'In 'Die Kunst der Fugue', for instance, he begins with four fugues, two of which introduce the subject-matter; the other two present it backwards; then there are counter-fugues where the pitches are flipped upside down and combined with the original music.'

61

'Holmes, you know perfectly well that I do not have the slightest clue about the technical side of music. I will take your word for it. Perhaps the message might be part of a crossword puzzle?'

'Or crossmusic puzzle? Who knows? Time for a proper pipe and then to work, Watson! What a way to spend Christmas Eve, eh?'

'Should we not invite Lily to join us?' I suggested. Our bright new housekeeper had already helped us on a couple of cases, in her ancillary role as a code-breaker.

'In a while, Watson. In a while. Let us see if we can break it together first, with you as my usual sounding board. After all, *we* are the detectives, and to my knowledge our housekeeper has not yet published a trifling monograph analysing one hundred and sixty ciphers, has she?'

After refilling our pipes, we sat down together at the table, with the thirty-two-letter puzzle set out in front of us:

GNKEWRUGFKCYHVGXUFRNURUMFKXUXKHL

'It is meaningless until it becomes meaningful, Watson. Let us begin with the simplest option. First of all I will draw a table with several columns, the letters of the Latin alphabet in the first column, and the letters of the code in the second column, like so.'

Holmes hastily pencilled a rough series of five columns, with thirty-two lines through them, and entered the two sequences:

A	G			
B	N			
C	K			
D	E			
E	W			

F	R			
G	U			
H	G			
I	F			
J	K			
K	C			
L	Y			
M	H			
N	V			
O	G			
P	X			
Q	U			
R	F			
S	R			
T	N			
U	U			
V	R			
W	U			
X	M			
Y	F			
Z	K			
	X			
	U			
	X			
	K			
	H			
	L			

'At first sight, there seems to be no logical relationship between the two columns.'

'That is clear even to me, Holmes.'

'Now let us include in the third column, the letters of the Latin alphabet, in reverse order,' enthused the great detective. 'This was a simple substitution cipher in the Hebrew language, known as the Atbash. It can be perceived in the Book of Jeremiah, Watson, in your beloved Old Testament. And many believe that it was used to disguise words in the Kabbalah, a school of thought originating in Judaism. A few English words can be Atbashed into other English words, such as *holy* and *slob*. Some other English words even Atbash into their own reverses, such as *wizard* for *draziw*.'

'All right, Holmes,' I sighed. 'I comprehend.'

Holmes worked his way rapidly down the table:

A	G	Z		
B	N	Y		
C	K	X		
D	E	W		
E	W	V		
F	R	U		
G	U	T		
H	G	S		
I	F	R		
J	K	Q		
K	C	P		
L	Y	O		
M	H	N		
N	V	M		
O	G	L		
P	X	K		
Q	U	J		
R	F	I		
S	R	H		
T	N	G		
U	U	F		
V	R	E		

W	U	D		
X	M	C		
Y	F	B		
X	K	A		
	X			
	U			
	X			
	K			
	H			
	L			

'That looks equally meaningless to me, Holmes. And it has nothing whatsoever to do with music.'

'Patience, Watson. Patience. We must now apply the message to the reversed alphabet, as follows. G becomes T, N becomes M, K becomes P, and so on.'

Holmes sketched his numbers into the table:

A	G	Z	T	
B	N	Y	M	
C	K	X	P	
D	E	W	V	
E	W	V	D	
F	R	U	I	
G	U	T	F	
H	G	S	T	
I	F	R	U	
J	K	Q	P	
K	C	P	X	
L	Y	O	B	
M	H	N	S	
N	V	M	E	
O	G	L	T	
P	X	K	C	

Q	U	J	F	
R	F	I	U	
S	R	H	I	
T	N	G	M	
U	U	F	F	
V	R	E	I	
W	U	D	F	
X	M	C	N	
Y	F	B	U	
X	K	A	P	
	X		A	
	U		F	
	X		A	
	K		P	
	H		S	
	L		O	

Now, Watson. What do you notice about the letters in the fourth column?'

'Nothing. More gobbledegook. Shall I call Lily?'

'You see, Watson. But you do not observe.'

Great God in heaven! How many more times would I have to listen to that tiresome complaint of his?

'Well, it is hardly obvious, is it?' I grunted.

'It is clear as a proverbial church bell to me. Let us go back one letter in the Latin alphabet each time, and then see what we have, shall we?'

He slotted a string of letters down the fifth column:

A	G	Z	T	S
B	N	Y	M	L
C	K	X	P	O
D	E	W	V	U
E	W	V	D	C
F	R	U	I	H

G	U	T	F	E
H	G	S	T	S
I	F	R	U	T
J	K	Q	P	O
K	C	P	X	W
L	Y	O	B	A
M	H	N	S	R
N	V	M	E	D
O	G	L	T	S
P	X	K	C	B
Q	U	J	F	E
R	F	I	U	T
S	R	H	I	H
T	N	G	M	L
U	U	F	F	E
V	R	E	I	H
W	U	D	F	E
X	M	C	N	M
Y	F	B	U	T
X	K	A	P	O
	X		A	B
	U		F	E
	X		A	B
	K		P	O
	H		S	R
	L		O	N

'Ah. So it is *not* a musical code. I was wrong. It is much simpler. And duller. Childish, almost. The meaning of the message is as follows:

SLOUCHESTOWARDSBETHLEHEMTOBEBORN,

or "*Slouches towards Bethlehem to be born*." ' Holmes sounded deeply disappointed.

'Yes. But what does *that* mean?' I queried.

'It is the last line of a poem by the Nobel prize-winning Irish poet, William Butler Yeats,' explained Holmes. 'Interestingly, a poem that is called *"The Second Coming."* '

'Good grief!' I gulped.

I was impressed by my colleague's gifts and literary knowledge, the product of so many lonely nights in his Sussex apiary. But I was also frightened. Could it be a message from God? Warning us about ....?

'Calm down, doctor,' smiled Holmes, reading my mind as usual. 'It is not a message from God. Why on earth would He use an Irish poet to communicate with us?'

'Because Yeats is a spiritualist,' I replied, wide-eyed. 'He also believes we can communicate with the dead. He was once a leading member of the Hermetic Order of the Golden Dawn, which I joined briefly after Bea's passing. Canon Thomas was born in Ireland. And because the Lord works in mysterious ways.'

'Yes, but not that mysterious, Watson,' laughed Holmes. 'Golden Dawn, indeed. More likely somebody playing games with the church organ. And for a definite reason, I'll lay a bet. Well. There's nothing more to be done here until the silver evening. Wake me up at 6pm, won't you? And don't bring your Service revolver. You won't need it.'

'I would not dream of bringing any weapon into a place of worship, Holmes. Besides, bullets are of little use on the astral plane,' I retorted.

But he had disappeared abruptly into his room without answering, leaving me alone to look forward to a night in a haunted church and a possible meeting with my Maker, without the dubious sustenance of a seven-per-cent solution of cocaine.

We descended from our hansom onto Cheyne Walk on the dot of eight. Stepping around a pile of fetid horse manure, we headed towards All-Saints Church through a thin whirling fog, which struggled to lift itself off the streets of London. The new electric street lights along the Chelsea Embankment cast a welcoming amber glow onto the stone masonry of its frontage as we turned up Old Church Street towards the side entrance.

Although the rain had ceased temporarily, the night air was still cold enough to generate other minor fogs from our separate breaths. The empty churchyard was silent, but for the distant hoot of a night owl and the scrunch of our footsteps upon the dead leaves. A phalanx of ghostly headstones in the darkened cemetery seemed to salute us as we passed by them and their surrounding gnarled bushes, into the side alcove, where we found a shivering Canon Thomas waiting anxiously for us.

'Thank God,' he said. 'You have made it. Everyone has gone home.' The vicar turned and opened the door into the vestry, the very room in which Holmes had explained to me the truth about the murder of his brother, Mycroft, in February of that same year.

'Well?' asked the vicar, once we were inside. 'The message?'

Holmes explained the meaning of the keyboard sequence to Canon Thomas, whose face blanched with fear at the mention of the Yeats poem.

'The Second Coming?' he cried. 'The Day of Vengeance? Surely it cannot be! We have not had the Rapture yet. Oh, my God! Maybe we have! And we were not included! Why, oh why, is this happening in *my* church?'

'Why not?' said Holmes ironically. 'It has to happen somewhere, if it is going to happen at all. Perhaps it's your lucky day. I suggest we adjourn to a point in front of the organ, so that we can view the ghostly coded message ourselves. Then we will be prepared for the musical interlude when it begins. Hurry up, Watson. Steel true, blade straight in the fight against true evil.'

'This is the House of God, Holmes,' I said. 'There can be no evil inside these walls.'

'You're sure of that, are you?' he replied, with a twinkle in his eye, as the Canon led us out of the vestry and into the body of the church. The clergyman was shaking in his shoes and muttering some words to himself from the Book of Revelation:

'And the beast was taken, and with him the false prophet that wrought miracles before him, with which he deceived them that had received the mark of the beast, and them that worshipped his image. These both were cast alive into a lake of fire burning with brimstone.'

The heavy odour of wax polish was mixed with the acrid fumes of cooling radiators and something else that I did not immediately recognise. It smelled like ... sulphur? *Brimstone?* Good Lord! My heart started jumping like a rabbit in response.

The limited degree of lighting came from the full moon outside the Harry Clarke stained-glass windows, and a few candles spread among the shadowy recesses at the sides. I removed a flashlight from the pocket of my ulster and switched it on. Its light pierced the murky interior and pointed up the nave past the pulpit and the eagle lectern, towards the chancel, beside which the organ pipes climbed upwards to the ceiling. An alarmingly life-like statue of Jesus Christ rose above the altar and gazed out blankly at the absent congregation.

Holmes reached the steps before the vicar – still whining away – and myself. I checked my watch at the top. It was 8.14. The vicar and I positioned ourselves expectantly in front of the Bevington organ. Waiting for 8.25 and Johann Sebastian.

But not Holmes. He had whipped out his magnifying lens and was stooping beneath the keyboard, examining the foot pedals at the base of the organ. Then he clambered energetically around the back, where he disappeared from our view for a while, reappearing at the other side just as my watch read 8.23, murmuring something to himself about wires.

Although we were prepared for the music two minutes later, when the Toccata started, it still managed to frighten the wits out of the vicar and myself. I was gratified to notice that even Holmes looked a little shaken. It was so loud that I imagined all living souls in Chelsea could hear it. Certainly I could not understand why the new vicar and his family did not come rushing across the road and into the church.

'There!' yelled the vicar suddenly, pointing to the lower keyboards. 'Do you see them? Do you see the letters, Mr. Holmes?'

The detective's lens was already flashing backwards and forwards across the white keys. Holmes chuckled to himself and turned abruptly to the vicar.

'Reverend. Would you please stand in front of the organ like ... so?' He positioned the agitated clergyman such that his body was leaning forward and covering the keyboard as much as possible.

71

'Now, Watson. Here is a test of your rational mind. What is the cause of these letters?' demanded Holmes. He was pointing at the vicar's back, on which a part of the message was clearly manifested.

'Obviously they are being projected in some way onto the keyboard. But from which direction?'

'From above, Watson. Straight down onto the organ. Look up. I suspect it is simply done. This dastardly business has been very carefully planned.'

Holmes was pointing up at the top of the pipes. I played my flashlight across the roof for several minutes before I spied the strip of white paper that stretched between the triangular tips of two organ pipes, with the light from the moon outside flickering through the diminishing fog and the letters etched into it.

'But why would someone do such a silly th ...?'

My question was interrupted by a loud groan from the clergyman, who was pointing towards the statue of Our Saviour in the chancel. I followed his stricken gaze to see the figure floating through the air towards us. I knelt down swiftly and bent my head in supplication, frozen with terror. Bach's Toccata had come to an end right at that very moment, almost like a signal from God. I started to say the Lord's Prayer. '*Our Father, which art in heaven, Hallowed be thy n...*'

But it was all too much for the poor vicar, who slumped off the keyboard and down onto the floor. I sensed Holmes moving swiftly to his side and feeling for a pulse in his neck.

'It is no good, Watson. Canon Thomas is beyond our help. I fear this feeble joke has now become ... an act of murder.'

'Who are you and what are you doing in my church?'

The commanding voice rang out clearly from the central aisle below the organ. I plucked up courage and raised my head slowly, to observe the statue of Jesus Christ on the Cross facing me, standing upright like a signpost to Golgotha in the hands of a black-bearded young man dressed in the purple Eucharistic vestments of an Anglican priest.

'My name is Sherlock Holmes, and this ... get up, man, get up ... this is Dr. John Watson.'

'Is that dear old Canon Thomas on the floor? Is he all right?' The voice had softened in genuine concern as the clergyman planted the statue against a pew and came towards us.

'No, sir,' replied Holmes, moving down the steps to face Canon Thomas' replacement. 'In point of fact, he is dead. And I fancy that you and your blessed offspring are to blame, and may face a charge of murder.'

'Murder? How dare you! What right have any of you to be inside the church at this hour? Even Canon Thomas himself should not be here. His wardenship came to an end when he retired this summer. But he would *keep* wandering around the place at night, moving hymnals and ringing bells whenever he felt like it. I really should have changed the locks on the doors.'

'Do you mean to suggest that you were not trying to deliberately frighten this poor man to death?' I asked, incensed at the callous attitude of the priest. 'What about the message on the organ? What about the Second Coming?'

'The Sec ...? What in God's name are you jabbering about? Blasphemer!'

'Why don't you come up here and see for yourself?' I shouted. Blasphemer, indeed. Me!

Holmes sat down suddenly upon a pew and started to giggle, as the new vicar approached the stairs.

'It is no laughing matter, Holmes! Canon Thomas is gone! He is dead!'

At this evidence of my rage, Holmes burst into uncontrolled chortling.

'I'm ... hee, hee, hee ... sorry, old chap. It is just that I ... hah, hah ... understand the whole business now. I think.' Holmes coughed, in a futile attempt to recover his gravitas. 'And ... and should not Canon Thomas be happy to have reached his final destination? To be in summerland? You really cannot have it both ways, Watson. You cannot look forward to an afterlife and then complain about it when you arrive there.'

Holmes started to giggle again. Soon I would have to talk to him about his return to the use of cocaine. It was unacceptable.

The new canon had reached the organ, taking care to step over the body of his predecessor. He stared in puzzlement at the message spread across the white keys.

'What does this mean? Where do these letters come from? And why do you call it the Second Coming?'

'It is a coded message that translates into a line from a poem called 'The Second Coming', by an Irish fellow called Yeats,' I replied heatedly. 'I'll have you know that it terrified the life out of Canon Thomas. This, together with the inexplicable playing of Bach's bloody Toccata for two minutes every night, caused him to call on the world's first consulting detective, the great Sherlock Holmes, for assistance in solving the case. And me. His assistant, Dr. Watson. Harrummpphh.'

'Thank you, Doctor. Not that it is any of your business, but I am experimenting with adapting our valuable old

Bevington organ into a system of electric recording for this church, in order to save money after Algernon leaves us for good at the end of the month. I am testing it every evening for two weeks, in order to satisfy myself that it will work according to a timed schedule during service. And you have not answered my question about the message and its origin.'

'Reverend, it would seem that one of your sons is a courageous climber, has an interest in mathematics and early ciphers, and studies the poetry of Yeats at school,' said Holmes from his pew. 'As well as being a deadly torment to poor old Canon Thomas. Why don't you look upwards. Watson, the flashlight.'

The vicar raised his head and stared up through the flashlight at the paper stream that fluttered across the pipes. He did not speak for about a minute as his eyes kept flicking back and forth between the paper and the organ keys. It seemed to me that the truth of what had happened was gradually beginning to dawn on him, as his hitherto ashen face turned an even paler shade.

'Great heavens above. I see how this happened. Paul. My eldest boy. It is his doing. He is a bright lad, but is never far away from some form of mischief. Always playing tricks on poor Canon Thomas. And the congregation. His favourite trick is to place rotten eggs underneath the pews to simulate brimstone. It is also true that my wife is currently struggling to get him interested in poetry. And Peter must be involved, else how could they have lined up the letters so accurately? Oh, please. Dear gentlemen! I do beg you to forgive my children for this.'

The deflated priest turned and held his arms out earnestly towards us.

'They must never know the results of their actions,' he implored. 'They are only schoolboys. It might damage their psyches permanently if they realised the good Canon's death had resulted from their game.'

The new cleric gazed forlornly from me to Holmes in abject hope.

'I believe they should be made aware of the dangers of their games, in order to avoid a possible repetition,' I replied. 'And I think they both may be guilty of manslaughter, rather than murder, and should be held to account before the law. What do you think, Holmes?'

Holmes stood up abruptly, as though bored with the whole affair.

'Watson, what earthly good would it do, if the lives of two playful, intelligent young boys were to be destroyed just to satisfy the contents of some clause in a legal document. It will not bring back Canon Thomas. If the Reverend would here and now promise to us that he discipline his sons for their dangerous games, and scrutinise their behaviour *much* more closely in future, I imagine that we could turn a blind eye to the foolish events of this evening. And he would also have to take care of Canon Thomas' remains, of course.'

'Certainly I will do all of that, Mr. Holmes. And thank you for understanding.'

'Please let us know the funeral arrangements at this address,' said Holmes briskly, handing his card to the cleric. 'Watson. Let us away. This is one story that I sincerely hope you refrain from documenting with that colourful and unreliable pen of yours.'

I did not agree with his attitude towards this particular crime, but when we had returned to 221B Baker Street and were smoking our last pipes of the day, Holmes mollified me somewhat by inviting me to take care of his cocaine needle and the supply of his drug, and to assist him in breaking his habit once again. I believe this case, or rather non-case, had led him to question his powers of detection. And to seek a return to a diet of Royal Jelly.

But he would go on and on about the subject of death and the afterlife.

'My dear Watson. It is my opinion that all religious beliefs are forms of necrophilia. To live one's life according to a set of rules that will enable the putative ascension into an imaginary Paradise at its end, to sit on the right-hand side of an imaginary God, as opposed to an intimidating scorching experience in the other place, is to be in love with death itself. That is what the unfortunate Canon Thomas was. A necrophile. A lover of death.'

Being too exhausted to argue, I refused the clear opportunity to claim that I might also be considered by that dreadful honorific. Never mind. Some day in the future I would convince him of the essential truth of spiritualism.

Holmes stretched his angular body lazily across the sofa, and yawned.

'As I said to you when we encountered the so-called Sussex vampire: *"This agency stands flat-footed upon the ground, and there it must remain. The world is big enough for us. No ghosts need apply".* '

4.   Sherlock Holmes And The Holland Park Cannibal.

'Have you ever thought of retiring, Holmes?' I asked my old friend and colleague one spring evening in 1926. 'From detecting, I mean? After all, you are seventy-two now, and I shall be entering my seventy-fifth year of life soon. We are getting on, you know.'

Holmes peered quizzically at me from around an array of Bunsen burners in the corner of our airy sitting room.

'Trust you to project your age into the future, Watson. You really should try to remain on seventy-three while you still can. And what would we do if we stopped? Sit around all day smoking our pipes and chatting about the good old cases? Moriarty, Moran and Milverton? Black Jack of Ballarat? No, old friend, my internal pump will cease to function after I have just solved an impossible murder and landed the culprit beneath a sturdy rope with a noose at its end! Such is the plan. A happy ending to a fruitful and fulfilling life. No summerland or winterland for me.'

His head disappeared behind the glass again.

'Huh!' I grunted. 'And murders are ten a penny nowadays, I suppose. Even possible ones.'

His reference to the spiritualist heaven and hell reminded me that it had been four months since the case of Canon Thomas' mysterious self-playing organ, which had led to the unfortunate clergyman's own pump ceasing to function in the Chelsea All-Saints Old Church, and a pyrrhic victory for Holmes' atheism over my belief in God. Apart from the facile business of the exploding Harrow cricket pavilion, which he solved in an afternoon without moving from his armchair, Holmes had experienced no case worthy of his energies since then.

Now it was my turn to be bored, as I did not possess the great detective's interest in all matters scientific, political and weird. I would skim past the newspaper reports of events in the House of Commons to get to the sports pages, or to read any columns of a military nature. I had exhausted accounts of the birth of the Duke of York's first daughter. Elizabeth is such a lovely name. I had even lost interest in medical issues, now that I no longer practised. My last patient had died a few weeks beforehand, of old age. He was one hundred and seven. There was little I could do for him.

My role in life was reduced to that of indispensable assistant to the world's first consulting detective. Holmes had returned to a daily seven-per-cent solution of cocaine after the disturbing case of the Hampstead ponies, but agreed subsequently that I could control the drug – hide it away, actually – and manage his rehabilitation by reducing the dose over a gradual period of time. He was down to two dosages a week by April 26th and remained supremely fit from a diet that included Royal Jelly. Once upon a time he had kept my cheque book locked in his desk to oversee my gambling habit and secure my wound pension, so I felt that I was returning a service as a friend.

'What are you up to over there?' I asked him. There was no reply.

'I said, "What are you doing over there?" '

'Eh, what? Did you say something, Watson?'

Holmes edged his way out from behind his chemistry table, pulled it back against the wall and joined me by the fireside, removing his apron and wiping his hands with some filthy towel.

'That new ultramicroscope you bought me for Christmas is providing endless hours of pleasurable study. Thank you again for it. Physics is almost as interesting a subject as Chemistry. I have just proven Heisenberg's matrix formulation of quantum mechanics for myself. We live in interesting times, Watson. His theory could alter the world of natural science as we know it. He is the successor to Newton and Einstein. I imagine it will win him a Nobel in the not too distant future.'

'Whose? What?'

'Let me get my pipe and explain it to you, old chap.'

Holmes grabbed his cherrywood from the coal-scuttle and rapped it several times against the hearth. Then he picked up his Persian slipper from the mantel, sat down and began to scoop tobacco out of it. He seemed to be mentally composing the scientific pamphlet with which he was about to bamboozle me. I had only myself to blame. Message for Dr. Watson. Keep mouth shut in future.

'It is rather complicated, but a medical man like yourself should be capable of understanding it. And don't worry. I shall try to keep the mathematics to a minimum. I know it is not your strong suit. Now. In terms of physics and very small things like the atom, Watson, *nothing is real unless it is observed.* Let me explain. The problem that faced Heisenberg was how to measure the position and momentum of electrons around the nucleus within each atom, as it was impossible to see *inside* an atom.'

Holmes sucked greedily on his pipe and blew a rapid series of perfect smoke rings towards the ceiling.

'I am sure you are aware that most ordinary matter is made up of atoms, whether it be a hansom cab, chair, book, pipe, egg, cat or human. Simply put, a human being is made of organ systems, organ systems are made of organs, organs are made of tissues, tissues are made of cells, cells are made of molecules and molecules are made of atoms.'

'And at the atomic level, I suppose all humans and animals are equal,' I stated.

'Of course. We are, after all, animals ourselves, Watson. Last year young Heisenberg became unhappy with the existing quantum theory of Bohr and company, which he felt did not fully explain the behaviour of light in several areas. Firstly, the study of light emitted and absorbed by atoms. Secondly, the predicted properties of atoms and molecules. Thirdly, the nature of light itself. Did it act like waves or like a stream of particles? So he set about replacing this old theory with one of his own. Since the electron orbits – their position and momentum – within atoms could not be observed, Heisenberg relied instead on what *could* be observed, namely the light emitted and absorbed by the atoms themselves. Are you following this, Watson?'

'What? Oh, yes, yes. With you so far. As you say, we doctors do have to study a bit of physics and chemistry at college.'

Mind you, I must admit that I had begun to drift into a rather pleasing anticipation of that evening's repast. Roast pork belly in red wine with crackling, buttered parsnips and baked rooster potatoes in their jackets, I believe Lily had suggested. Plenty of lovely juicy atoms there.

'At first Heisenberg struggled to find a means of measuring even this light, due to the changing positions of the elements within the atoms. Then he decided to experiment with symbols as *imaginary* quantities within arrays of numbers, called *matrices*. The rules for calculating these symbols depend on the order they are written down, as well as their inherent value. So if you multiplied one matrix called **p** (position) by another called **q** (momentum), the result would be a third matrix, a possible measurement. But if you multiplied **q** (momentum) by **p** (position), the result would be a different matrix, also a possible measurement. This trial and error experiment worked, although he could not understand *why* it worked. It became known as 'matrix mechanics.' Subsequently, with the help of several other physicists, he was responsible for developing a new theoretical quantum mechanics that could account for many of the properties of atoms and atomic events. You do see what this means for our profession, don't you, Watson?'

'Eh, not quite, no,' I replied. With cherry-raspberry buckle and vanilla ice cream for dessert.

'It is a vital step on the path to our full understanding of human life, down to the ultimate level within the atoms that we are made of. The smallest of the small.'

Holmes waved his pipe around in excitement.

'Some day, Watson, just as we can now identify criminal suspects through the capture of their unique fingerprints, it will be possible for a forensic detective to establish beyond any reasonable doubt, the presence of a murderer at his crime scene by harvesting his unique atomic identity. Admittedly, in a way that is unknown to me at present.'

'Then people like you and I will be out of a job, won't we, Holmes? The police will be able to solve all the crimes themselves.'

The great detective was silent as his hawklike features processed this little nugget of mine. His face flushed with annoyance at first, then looked slightly puzzled, and finally creased into a smile of genuine admiration.

'Watson, my dear fellow. I do believe you have hit the nail on the head. The days of the consulting detective are numbered. Fortunately it will be many years after the return of our own atoms to the soil before this happens. But hopefully the discovery will come in time to destroy the careers of that preening Poirot and the effete Lord Peter Wimsey. Hah! I have been too interested in the methodology itself to realise its full implications. Well done, old fellow!'

My heart warmed at the praise of a man of the stature of Sherlock Holmes. Rarely did I occupy the intellectual high ground in his presence, and I basked joyfully in it, only to be interrupted by the familiar clump, clump clump of our housekeeper's clodhoppers upon the stairs. These were followed by a less familiar set of footfalls, which belonged to Jasper Lestrade, son of our deceased nemesis George, and a young Scotland Yard detective of considerable promise and great assistance to us in our recent investigations. He had proposed marriage to Lily over Christmas, she had accepted, and I had recklessly volunteered to give her away at their autumn nuptials.

'Jaispair an' oi wur wonnerin' if yer coul' 'elp us, Mr. 'Olmes.'

Lily was obviously in a very bad state, red-eyed and wringing her hands on her apron in distress. I helped her onto the basket-chair, while Holmes and Lestrade sat together on the sofa.

The younger Lestrade was not quite as ferret-faced as his father. Nevertheless many rabbits would scarper in terror if he was sent in after them. That trim black pencil moustache, almost hidden by his gargantuan aquiline nose, served only to emphasize the ghostly pallor of his skin. His adenoidal squeak was manifestly unsuited to a serious Scotland Yard detective. It lacked gravity. I found myself happily anticipating the transformation of his healthy lean frame into an oval-shaped egg over the next few years of Lily's cooking. What, me? Jealous?

'It is a good friend of Lily's, Mr. Holmes. A maid. She seems to have disappeared. Noone has seen her for three days. We thought you might be able to investigate ...'

'Of course, of course,' Holmes interrupted. 'Do tell me. What is the name of this woman, and when was she last seen alive?'

Lily blew her nose stridently. ''er naime's Mowreen O'Roilly, an' we been pals fer doinkey's yairs. We was a' skuhle togethair. She wur tah meet me on 'er day orff laist Tewesday at the 'olland Park tea rewmes, but she navair toined up.'

'And where does Maureen work?' I enquired.

'She is a maid to the Carstairs family,' explained Lestrade.

'Is that Lord William Carstairs, the current Secretary of State for the Colonies and Dominions?' asked Holmes.

'Indeed it is. Apparently she left the house – they live in the Royal Crescent – that Tuesday morning, but never reached the tea rooms. I have since talked to Mrs Carstairs, and she is also most concerned. Scotland Yard has added Maureen to its list of missing persons. A description has gone out to all uniformed police on duty.'

Lestrade started to pat Lily's hand in an effort to comfort her, but she pulled it away from him.

'Oi fink ahnley yer an' Watsey can foind 'er, Mr. 'Olmes. She ... she's a bit bleedin' woild, yer know. Loikes 'er blowkes, she does. She'd troi anyfink once, she wud. Oi fink she migh' be daid.'

Holmes leant forward eagerly on the sofa.

'Why do you think that, Lily?' he asked.

'Jes' a feelin', oi s'pose. Nofink speshail.'

'Have you examined the gardens of the Carstairs house, Lestrade?' enquired Holmes.

'Certainly, Mr. Holmes. We found nothing. It was the same with the neighbours all along the Crescent. Needless to say, we have not dug up every inch of soil, as these are mature lawns, with no sign of disturbance. Also the occupants would not take kindly to it, as they belong to what my late father used to call the *powerful* class.'

'And pray, what is at the bottom of the garden?'

'Just some old stables. They are not used now,' answered Lestrade.

'What about the communal garden in front of the crescent?' I suggested.

'Nothing there either. It is a mystery. She seems to have vanished off the face of the earth,' muttered Lestrade.

'That is easy enough to do in a city like London. If you wish to, that is. Was she happy in her work?' asked Holmes.

'Yeah. Oi fink so. 'appy 'nuff.'

'Did she have a particular boyfriend?' I asked. 'One that she might consider eloping with?'

'Nah. She loved 'em an' laift 'em, did Mowreen. She 'ad noone nahw.'

'What about family and other friends? Girls, I mean?' I persisted.

85

'Nah, Watsey. She wur an ahnly child. 'er ma an' da're undair the sod. She nevair menshunned othair frien's.'

'Who else lives at the Carstairs residence?' enquired Holmes.

'Just an old butler with Lord and Lady Carstairs. The four children have all left home,' replied Lestrade.

'Watson, I fancy a visit to the domicile of the Secretary of State might be called for,' said Holmes, hoisting himself off the sofa and straightening his waistcoat. 'Immediately. The sooner we depart, the better for all concerned. Lestrade, you must come with us. Do not worry, Lily. We will find your friend for you.'

'What about dinner, Holmes?' I enquired, knowing that such a question was futile.

'Watson, Watson. Forever thinking of your stomach. You will not starve. Have you not eaten already today?'

The Royal Crescent had been designed in 1839 as part of the Norland Estate. It was not planned in the exact shape of a lunula, but rather as two quadrant terraces, each terminated by a circular bow tower in the Regency style. Although the idea had been to copy the older Bath crescent, architectural aesthetics had to play second fiddle to the need for the newly fashionable underground sewers, a must for the Crescent's well-to-do London occupants.

These facts were communicated to us by the ever knowledgeable Holmes as our brougham meandered lazily down Holland Park Avenue towards our sickle-shaped destination.

The Carstairs residence was situated in the centre of the first of the two quadrants. We were greeted at the door and ushered into a palatial living room by Lady

Dorothea Carstairs herself. She was an imposing plump lady in her sixties, with greying hair pinned up in a bun, a severe dark green bustled dress that covered her entire rectangular frame right down to her sensible brown shoe-straps, and a set of canines that would frighten the life out of passing horses and drown any humans who stood too close to her.

'Have you found my dear Maureen yet?' she slurped imperiously at Lestrade, who flinched.

'No, ma'am. But we will. Have no fear on that. May I introduce Mr. Sherlock Holmes, and this is his colleague, Dr. Watson.'

'How do you do? Please sit,' commanded our upper class host. Lestrade and I obeyed immediately. Her voice reminded me of my years as an army surgeon, both in Afghanistan and later on in France. My leg twinged sharply in harmony with thoughts of that second Afghan War. Although the limb of this old campaigner still contained bits of a jezail bullet from the Battle of Maiwand, for some time it had not bothered me, even when the weather changed. Until now.

But Holmes was her equal in arrogance and moved leisurely over to the rear window. He took in every detail as he gazed out at the back garden and paused before replying, to emphasize his control of the situation.

'Does your maid live in, and if so, may we examine her room?' he enquired, eventually.

Lady Carstairs looked bewildered for a moment, as though the idea of a maid having accommodation of her own would be inconceivable.

'Of course she lives with us, sir,' she sprayed. 'How else would she be able to serve us when we need her?

And if you refuse to sit down, we might as well adjourn to her room right away.'

'Lady Carstairs, I beg you to point us in the general direction of her quarters, and then leave us to do our work, if you would not mind,' said Holmes, smiling coldly.

Lady Carstairs' face turned from pink to puce in a split second and her eyes narrowed to tiny slits like pencil lines.

'Well, really! In my own house! What is the world coming to? Just who do you think you are?'

'That is a simple question, which has already been answered. I am Sherlock Holmes. The room?'

I could see that Holmes was enjoying this little contretemps, but Lady Carstairs looked fit to burst the seams of her corset.

'You will wait here until the butler arrives, and he will then show you to Maureen's room,' she squirted.

With this futile attempt to regain the upper hand, the matron stormed out of the room, like a damaged galleon in full retreat upon the high seas. Within a minute she was replaced by a stately old boy with shaking liver-spotted hands, who looked the epitome of loyal servanthood, and must have been at least ninety years of age. His name was Jenkins and he led the three of us sedately down a set of rickety stairs, through a kitchen and into a damp corridor. He stopped outside an open door, nodded his head at us, raised his sketchy white eyebrows, grinned knowingly, and vanished.

Holmes the bloodhound materialized once inside the room, opening drawers, riffling through their contents, peering into the wardrobe, examining clothes, sniffing the pillows and bedsheets and the contents of the maid's dressing table. These included a photo, an old vase of wilting hyacinths, some cheap pieces of jewelry and a musical trinket box, which played '*Twinkle Twinkle Little Star*' while he rummaged around inside until he came across a small yellow clothes tag. He held it up to the light.

'Ah. Most interesting,' he commented, placing it in his pocket. He perused the framed photo of the missing girl for a brief moment and then proceeded to clean his magnifying glass vigorously with a handkerchief, before stretching down on the floor to examine the damp wooden timbers minutely. Even under the bed.

Maureen's was a small, mean room when compared to the luxury upstairs, but I supposed that it was some sort of refuge for her from the demands of the Carstairs family. It certainly did not compare favourably to Lily's 'slave quarters' at 221B Baker Street. But then I really could not imagine what the life of a maid might be like.

Holmes stood up abruptly and pocketed his lens.

'Where does this lead to, I wonder?' he asked, pointing at a discoloured wallpapered door in the wall.

'Nowhere,' replied Lestrade. 'It is a dummy door. Just for show, I think.'

Holmes tapped twice against the door, and then twice against the wall. The sounds were identically hollow. He moved over to examine the window and curtains, before turning brusquely to us.

'Yes. She would not have wanted to be observed, so she must have gone out through the garden, via the kitchen door. Well, gentlemen, I think that I have seen all that I need to see. There is nothing more to do tonight. We need not trouble Sir William. I imagine that he is a busy man and frequently absent from his home. Lily's young friend has been either kidnapped or murdered. As it is not in the wardrobe, I think we can assume that she was wearing a purple beaded taffeta dress of the kind so popular with ... what is the word? ... ah, yes, flappers, I believe they are called. The interesting question is how a mere maid could afford to purchase such an expensive item from Harrods. She was also wearing three-inch high-sheeled shoes and probably a dark blue cloche hat, which is also missing. Undoubtedly she was going to meet her benefactor under the guise of having tea with Lily. It is that person we must find.'

'But how, Holmes?' I asked.

'Tomorrow morning first thing, you will travel to Harrods with this ticket ...' here he handed me the stub from his pocket '... and establish when the dress was sold, and who bought it. Bring a copy of the photo of Miss O'Reilly that the police are using. I have other things to attend to. I strongly suspect that the next item on our agenda will be the discovery of her body. Let us depart.'

Holmes was uncannily accurate in his prediction. Lestrade arrived at Baker Street before lunch the following day with the news that a naked female body had been washed up during the night in a sewage pumping station at Abbey Mills, south of Hackney. Lady Carstairs had identified it tearfully as belonging to her maid, Maureen O'Reilly. The Scotland Yard detective took it upon himself to give Lily the bad news, and left us to contemplate this not unexpected development.

'What do you make of the missing parts of her body, Holmes?' I asked. Jasper had informed us of some fairly gruesome details about the corpse. Maureen's eyes had been pulled out, and both buttocks and one thigh were missing slices of her flesh.

The great detective was brooding and had lit the foulest of his pipes, which he was smoking assiduously.

'I do not make anything of them yet. I never surmise without the full facts, as you very well know. We shall have to wait until the autopsy tomorrow to find out how she died. We can only hope that Jack the Ripper has not resurfaced. How did you get on at Harrods?'

'Just let me open a window first. There, that's better!'

I sat down beside the aperture to avail of the slightly fresher smog from Baker Street.

'Very well, I believe. A lady there identified the dress from the tag and asked her colleagues if any of them knew who had bought it. I showed the photograph to a very pretty salesgirl, who was adamant that she had sold it to a young lady a week ago, but not to the young lady in the photograph.'

'Ah!' exclaimed Holmes. 'Excellent! Well done! Progress! And did you get a description of this mysterious other young lady?'

'Yes, but it may not be of any use. The girl remembered her because of her strange attire. *She looked like a concubine from a harem.* Her words, Holmes. Let me see. I made some notes.'

I licked my finger and flicked rapidly through my Walker's pocket diary.

'Here we are. *She was veiled and wearing a white blouse and pleated khaki harem pants.*'

'Harem pants. Hah! Whatever will they think of next?'

'I don't know. Short skirts, maybe?'

'Explain, Watson.'

'These pants are *large and baggy and loose fitting, puffy even, with elastic at the waist and ankles.* Again, just quoting. The salesgirl, who had seen a picture show about Egypt once, thought that she looked like an off-duty belly-dancer.'

'But she was veiled. That is the important word, Watson. *Veiled.* For a reason, no doubt. The salesgirl cannot identify her. In point of fact, she may even have been Maureen herself.'

'That is correct.'

'Yet it is an excellent disguise for a murderess, don't you think? I suppose your lady friend was certain that it was a woman?'

'I asked her that very question, Holmes. She thought for a few seconds, and replied candidly that the glossy blonde hair could easily have been a wig, but her customer did have a bosom of enviable proportions and was also wearing a pair of black Arabic sandals, with purple toe-nails sticking out of them. And she looked ... overweight.'

'Hhmm. Indicative, but hardly conclusive. What colour were her eyes?'

'Eh, I didn't get that.'

'Pity. So the only real clue we have, apart from the state of the victim's body, resides within the sewers of London. According to Lestrade, it had travelled along the Lower Level Sewer before its arrival at the Northern Outflow at Abbey Mills, and could have been dumped into it at any point along the way, some time within the last four days. The autopsy will provide a more accurate time of death, but we cannot wait for that. Action is required now. Fortunately I keep an up-to-date Bazalgette map of the London sewer system within my arcane library in the corner. It should show us all the entry points into the Lower Level. Can you get it for me, old chap? Since Lily reorganised my data it is fiendish hard to find anything there.'

Holmes steepled his fingers under his chin and gazed complacently into deep space.

'Poor Lily,' he continued. 'We must find her friend's killer, Watson. Her murderer, or murderess.'

The old chap dutifully thumbed his way patiently through a phalanx of dictionaries, indices, notebooks, files and newspaper cuttings.

'Why don't you throw all this stuff around the place like you used to, Holmes?' I complained. 'Create a tremendous clutter? Then I wouldn't have to ... oh, this looks like it.'

'Good man. Let us explore it together.'

Holmes grabbed the document from me and spread it across the table, peering intensely at the complicated diagram. To my mind it looked like a map of the Underground Railway, with thick lines being criss-crossed by thin lines, and the bulbous Thames curving through the middle like a python.

'You do realise, Watson, that we would both probably be dead from cholera by now, but for this far-sighted fellow?'

'Yes, I am well aware of the achievements of Sir Joseph Bazalgette, Holmes. We doctors do know a little about matters that used to affect the nation's health. But you should also credit the novelist Charles Dickens, who started a single-minded war on London filth within his books, most notably "Bleak House".'

'Really? You are a fund of information, Watson. I must read it some time when I have a spare month.'

Thankfully my colleague had put his foul pipe to one side and I could breathe safely at his side, as he began to trace the possible last journey of Maureen O'Reilly along the Lower Level Sewer back to the area of the Royal Crescent.

'Let us assume that she was dumped somewhere near to where she lived, as her high heels and fancy dress would suggest a short journey. Ah, here we are:

The area covering the central portion of the Holland Ward and parts of the southern section of the Norland and Pembridge Wards: The Council's sewer meets the Counters Creek sewer near Royal Crescent and requires relief at a point near Holland Park Avenue/Norland Square junction.'

'Well, Watson? Do you fancy a trip to Counters Creek sewer? Followed by a spot of exercise strolling through the real London underground?'

Holmes was grinning at me so manically that I wondered if I had hidden his cocaine stash in a sufficiently safe place.

'Certainly not. I am far too old for wading through excrement. You will have to bring Lestrade. I will remain here and console Lily.'

'Watson! Where is that sterling doggedness of yours? The famous couragous tenacity? That steadfast loyalty your readers are so fond of? Your sense of right and wrong? What would your old colleagues in the Fifth Northumberland Fusiliers say? Leave young Jasper with his bride-to-be. She is naturally upset. Do not argue. Come along, Watson. Look to your laurels. There is not a moment to lose. Vital clues could be swishing their way down the sewers as we speak, and our fat murder ... ess might be planning her next killing at this very moment. Bring a flashlight, a pair of wellington boots and a handkerchief to hold over your nose. And it might be advisable if you primed that old Service revolver of yours and slid it into your pocket.'

As usual I could find no valid counterargument to Sherlock Holmes when he was in this bullish mood, and so one hour later we found ourselves heaving up a manhole cover in the middle of St. Ann's Road – growlers and taxis having been halted by the police – and clambering down a metal ladder into the stinking bowels of London's earth.

'Good Lord,' I muttered, as we stood together in a long brick-lined tunnel that led off in three directions. Even with a hanky over my face, the stench was overpowering. Holmes' shag tobacco was the very perfume of hyacinths in comparison. But it was a relief to see that we could walk along the side of the passage, without having to wade through the central gulley, where the slimy effluent swilled and gurgled along happily.

'Straight ahead, Watson,' suggested Holmes. 'We do not want to end up at the Chelsea Embankment.'

Although he had trained himself many years earlier to see in the dark, Holmes used my flashlight to read more details from his map description as we walked. His voice echoed eerily down the cavern.

'Bazalgette's brilliant idea had been to construct eighty two miles of underground brick main sewers to intercept sewage outflows – we are walking along part of that – and eleven hundred miles of street sewers to intercept the raw sewage which until then flowed freely through the London Streets. The outflows were pumped downstream into the Thames, well to the East of the city itself, and thence out to the sea. Although it had not been a part of his plan, and against much opposition from vested interests, who felt the sewage made for good fertiliser along the banks of the Thames, he succeeded in wiping out the cholera infection altogether, as well as getting rid of 'The Big Stink'. And that was over sixty years ago, Watson. Because he made these sewers so wide, the system will probably last forever, no matter how many people move to the capital.'

'What are we looking for, Holmes?' I asked, having quite lost interest in the history of London faeces and urine some time ago. 'If she was naked when thrown into this foul gutter, what clues can we possibly find?'

'I do not know, Watson. But if we can find out *where* she was injected into the system, we might then have a lead to where her killer lives. Be patient, man. And do try to keep up.'

Holmes strode forcefully through the central sludge, not caring how much his clothes were tainted by the corrupt fluid. I remained on the ledge behind him. As we progressed, a thunderous roar grew in volume and threatened to burst our eardrums. It was the sound of running water, swelling towards us through our subway.

'What is that vile cacophony, Holmes?' I shouted.

'It is the Counters Creek River, culverted beneath the streets of London many years ago, just like the Fleet, the Tyburn and the Westbourne,' he yelled back. 'It runs through this sewer up ahead. Don't worry. There will be a path over it.'

The polluted river churned its noisome way across the sewer through a wide runnel with a small railed bridge that we could just about edge across, although effluent slapped around our ankles. It had obviously been culverted to assist in the movement of sewage over to the Chelsea Embankment pumping station, as its odour challenged that of the sewer itself. Yet I noticed one or two small fish still struggling to survive within its ruddy moil.

'Here we are,' shouted Holmes, after we had travelled a few yards beyond the river. 'Let us examine this first entry point. Take your flashlight and shine it over there, will you?'

Holmes pointed to the ground beneath the steps and proceeded to do his famous impression of a hungry bloodhound in the light of the flashlight.

'Hhmm. Not much here, I'm afraid. Just shine it on the steps so I can check them also.'

'Yes, but whoever did this awful deed would have had to ensure that the body was taken away by the central ... flow, would they not?' I suggested.

'Good point, Watson. And they might have climbed down the steps to do so, and left a possible clue. So shine away up here.'

Holmes disappeared into the entrance chute and tried to push open the grille. It wouldn't budge, and he slipped back down.

'That has not been opened in many a long year. On to the next one.'

And the next one, and the one after that, and the one after that, and then ...

'What have we here?' asked Holmes. 'Shine the flashlight, Watson.'

Blood. Definitely blood. Red. Not a pool of the stuff, but a thin sliver that sneaked along the rivets in the ground below the steps.

'She was flung down here,' said Holmes excitedly. 'Look. The blood goes right up to the edge of the gulley. Where are we? Flashlight, please?'

He held up the diagram to my light and perused it closely.

'Ah, yes. Here we are. Remember this, Watson. It is Norland Square. If the grille up here moves easily, we will have more evidence.'

He leapt up the ladder like a tiger chasing a zebra. His hands gripped the manhole cover and he pushed it upwards so easily that it clanged back noisily onto the road above, wrenching his arm forward.

'This is it!' he cried, rubbing his wrist. 'Come, Watson. The game is afoot. Move those lazy atoms of yours!'

We emerged from the filthy tunnel to find ourselves standing in the middle of a strangely quiet road, directly outside number 40 Norland Square. The air was like oxygen to my mind, it was so refreshingly clean in comparison to the sewer.

'All right, Holmes,' I gulped. 'But she could hardly have been dumped down there in broad daylight. Even at night the killer would have been taking a significant risk, with the street lamps, would he not?'

'Maybe. Maybe not. Depends how it was done. There's no sign of blood on the road around the grille. She may have been carried in a blanket or bag. She may even have been alive when she was dumped.'

'Oh, I do hope not,' I said.

'Now, to work. With a bit of luck nobody of interest has seen us emerging from the sewer. We will become beggars, Watson. Veterans of the war effort, Major. Down on our luck. We smell like them already, do we not? Here, smear this mud on your face. Turn your jacket inside out, like ... so. And pull your tie off to the side, like ... that. Open your shirt and your flies.'

'My flies?'

'Just do as I say! Where's that famous limp of yours? Bring it out to play. Oh, very good. I'd give you a half-crown myself. Let us start at the end of this side of Norland Square, bearing in mind the houses nearest to the drain may provide the best clues. Otherwise the killer might have been seen dumping poor Maureen.'

And so began our short, unsuccessful career as professional beggars, caps in outstretched hands, looking for 'a little bit of 'elp in these 'ard times, ma'am', a cockney accent being the best that I could manage at short notice. A deranged Holmes had transformed himself miraculously by rumpling his thick mass of grey hair, twisting his face into a damaged rictus, turning in his toes and bending his back, as though he had been run over by a Beardmore taxi. While we awaited dismissals out of hand, doors shut in our faces, a choice oath or two and a spare bob here or there, we focussed our eagle eyes upon whoever answered the door, and the hall inside.

We had managed to harbour a few meagre coins, but nary a single pointer to Maureen's killer by the time we arrived back at number 40. There the door was opened by an extraordinarily beautiful young woman with bouncing chestnut curls, who could not have been more than twenty-five years of age, and who bestowed upon us one of the sweetest smiles that my aged melting heart had ever encountered.

'You poor darlings,' she purred, flicking a drooping ringlet away from her eyes with a delicate, floury hand. 'Please do come in. You look like you could eat a hearty meal. My name is Cynthiah Fitzwilton, by the way. Cynthiah. Spelled with two *aitches*.'

Her accent contained more than a hint of broad Australian, but it was a delicate violin compared to the one that followed.

'Och aye, Miss Fitzwilton, wi' a brace o' ai'ches,' grovelled my fellow beggar. 'We's got stomac's lake wee 'oles in snow. This pore minger's Stuart, an' ye can cawll me browken Bruce.'

The speed with which Holmes had dropped into some obscure Scots dialect was truly impressive. Where did he get his brogues from, I wondered? Did he have a library of them stored somewhere in that overcrowded cerebral cortex of his, that he could dip into whenever they were needed?

I limped docilely after him through a narrow hallway, which led down a few steps into a capacious, steam-filled scullery-kitchen. Holmes dragged his leg after him along the uneven flagstones in a way that made my dainty hobble look like a twitch.

The room was suffocatingly hot, due to a raging coal fire in the corner that fed its heat into a huge old-fashioned step-top cooking range beside it. Yet our hostess seemed as cool as sliced cucumber to me.

'Please sit at the table, boys, and I'll bring your food over. I'm studying to be a chef and have just made these sausages this morning. They're nice and fresh. There's no mash, but I'll cut you some bread. I have some soup on also, but it's not quite ready yet.'

While the elegant Miss Fitzwilton was busy at the stove, I noticed that Holmes had relaxed his twisted gait slightly. His eyes acquired their customary fierce glare as he scanned the kitchen swiftly for possible clues, missing

100

nothing. He seemed particularly interested in a half-open pantry door off the scullery, that led to another set of stairs. Then he strained forward to get a better view of the back garden through the window. Yet when she turned around with two plates for us, he had slipped back immediately into his damaged Scottish persona.

'Och, Miss Fitzwil'on, bonnie bangers an' bap, jes' wha' the docktur ordurred, ye wee magic lassie.'

'Let me get your cutlery,' she replied.

'Ta ever so, Miss Sinthya,' I added in my best cockney slang. Anything Holmes could do, I could do just as well. And I saw no reason why a poor beggar could not have good manners, even if my mendicant companion did not.

'Eat away, you absolute dears.'

It was true that I was ravenous. As I had not yet had lunch, I tucked voraciously into the three plump, delicious-looking sausages on my plate. It must have seemed to the wonderfully sympathetic Miss Fitzwilton that I was exactly the starving beggar I was supposed to be.

I had just finished the first one – they had such an unusual taste that I found myself wondering whether pork or veal formed the main ingredient – and had begun to chew upon the second, when I was interrupted by an almighty explosion from the front door, as though it had been blown off its hinges, followed by a rapid crunching of boots along the hall and towards our makeshift canteen.

It was as though a mad bull had invaded our terrain. If someone asked me to describe the stocky, sweating, beetroot-faced character who stood upon the steps down to the kitchen, whip in right hand, jacket, hat, breeches, jodhpurs, the full complement of riding gear, I would have simply answered, 'Grimesby Roylott', from an earlier Holmes case called 'The Speckled Band'. I seemed to recall that it involved a snake and a whistle, but it was so long ago, and my memory, not being what it was ...?

'How many times have I asked you not to entertain these sorts of ... *smelly* tramps in my house, Cynthiah?' he roared, in an accent that came straight from the Australian outback, and transformed Roylott into old Black Jack Of Ballarat from 'The Boscombe Valley Mystery.'

'Oh, but papa,' she wailed. 'They looked so hungry and down and out.'

'Out is what they are now, right enough,' growled her father, advancing towards the table, tapping his whip gently up and down upon his left hand in a way that looked distinctly threatening to me. 'Come on, you two. On your way.'

I caught Holmes' short jerk of the head as a signal to leave, and reluctantly stood up with as much dignity as a man with open flies could summon.

'Let's awa', wee Stew,' groaned Holmes, lifting his twisted body off the seat. 'Yon scunner nae want us in his hoose'.

I followed my fellow beggar as he dragged his body slowly up the steps and along the hallway. Just as we reached the door, Miss Fitzwilton came running after us, and pressed a package into my hand.

'That's the rest of the uneaten sausages,' she whispered. 'I'm sorry about my father. He is very nervous of strangers since we returned from living abroad. Best of luck to you both. Here, let me open the door.'

We maintained our act outside until we reached number 34 and Miss Fitzwilton had disappeared inside her house. Then Holmes straightened himself up, dusted his suit down and ran his fingers briskly through his hair.

'Mark my words, Watson. Next time we meet up with our jockey friend Fitzwilton, I shall remember to bring my life preserver with me,' he said quietly. 'A sound thrashing wouldn't go amiss there.'

'I'll come with you,' I agreed, thinking about having another sausage after they had cooled down sufficiently.

'Well! Did you see it?' he demanded excitedly.

'See what?'

'The *veil*, Watson,' he spat angrily. 'The veil that was hanging on the hall-stand.'

'Oh, but Holmes, surely you don't think that lovely young lady would have anything to do with murder, do you?'

'Why not?' he replied. 'Some of history's most vicious criminals have been young ladies. And whether they are beautiful or not is irrelevant. What are they like inside? That is the question. And don't eat any more of those sausages. You don't know what has gone into the making of them. I didn't touch mine.'

'Would you like one now?' I asked him, opening the bag.

'No, thank you, Watson. I have no wish to become a cannibal.'

The full force of Holmes' words only struck me as I was swallowing the remainder of my second sausage.

'A *cannibal*?' I choked.

'Yes, Watson,' Holmes. 'Our killer is a *cannibal*. It is the only explanation for the missing body parts. I did some reading up on the subject this morning. I am sorry to break this news to you at such an inopportune moment, old friend. I know it will be difficult for you. But you need to know, in order to progress the case. Those sausages might just contain bits of Lily's friend. Fortunately the soup wasn't ready, as apparently human eyes make quite a decent broth.'

I had already begun to vomit up my lunch before he had finished. As I slumped onto the pavement, I realised that I must have had a subliminal inkling of this fact, as I accepted his appalling suggestion without question, merely a quiet groan. What abominations were we humans capable of? Was there no limit to our fiendishness?

'But why didn't you *warn* me, Holmes?' I demanded, wiping my mouth.

'Because I wanted to see your reaction. Calm down, old fellow. It is just an outdated taboo. Here is a definitive question for you,' said Holmes, sitting down beside me. 'If you had nothing else to eat, and the alternative was starving to death, would you eat human flesh? Properly cooked, of course? With a decent pepper sauce and a few boiled carrots and potatoes?'

I turned around and stared at my friend, aghast.

'Absolutely not. It is against all that I hold dear in life,' I replied. 'Against God. You may laugh, Holmes, but I would genuinely rather starve to death. Especially if I had carrots and potatoes to hand. I came close to that unhappy state in the Afghan business all those years ago, when I had to do without food for a couple of weeks, due to enteric fever. No. I would not be able to enter my house justified, if I had broken that particular proscription. Oh, God! And now I have, all unknowing!'

I flung the package into the gutter angrily.

'Watson. It is not yet certain that Cynthiah Fitzwilton is a cannibal. Although I strongly suspect that she purchased the new outfit for Maureen O'Reilly, disguised as an odalisque. But why would she do such a thing, I wonder? This case grows more complicated by the minute.'

He paused as he bent forward to tie up a shoelace. 'Hopefully we shall never have to find an honest answer to that question of mine. My feeling is that we are all savages in the end. Our civilization is but a thin veneer that would disappear rapidly without the food chain. You were helpless in Afghanistan, but if you had a chance of survival, and could grasp it, you would do so. Our world is based upon the survival of the fittest, Watson. Believe me, there is *nothing* else. *Nothing.* And meat is meat. Just a collection of atoms. Apparently human meat tastes a little like pork. But I am equally sure your God would have forgiven you.'

'Would he? I doubt that, Holmes. I really do,' I moaned. 'Actually, I feel quite ill now.'

'Cheer up, old man,' said Holmes, standing up. 'Let us return to Baker Street. I would like to find out more about our friend Fitzwilton from my indices. Did you notice the photo of himself in mufti upon the kitchen wall? No. I thought not. You see, Watson, but you do ... etc., etc., Part of the caption read New Guinea – one of the few countries in the world where the practice of eating your fellow man is deemed acceptable. Pick up those sausages. I'm sure Lestrade will want to examine them. Later on tonight, we will pay another visit to number 40, and find out a bit more.'

'Oh, Lord. We're not going to have another break-in, are we, Holmes?' I pleaded.

A break-in was exactly what he planned, just as it had been all those years before at the dastardly blackmailer Charles Augustus Milverton's house, but not one that involved your esteemed narrator. The thought that I might have eaten part of the body of Lily's best friend, albeit unwittingly, combined with the journey through that filthy sewer, was too much for my aging body. After a hot bath, I was forced to retire to my upstairs room for the night, leaving Holmes to continue his manic investigation in the company of Wiggins, the last of the original Baker Street Irregulars, and the only one to have avoided a prolongued internment courtesy of Her Majesty's Prison Service. The world's first consulting detective filled me in on the details after we had breakfasted the following morning.

'Fortunately there was only a tiny sliver of moon, and we could make our way under cover of the night's cloak down the narrow lane to the rear of Norland Square,' recounted Holmes, enjoying his morning dottles pipe.

'I had perceived a gate at the bottom of the garden, Watson, which Wiggins opened with considerable ease. The scoundrel wanted five pounds for the night. I gave him two. A lot more than a shilling! Yet he is surely a loss to the criminal world, with his lock breaking skills. The window into the scullery yielded in much the same way, and by the time one o'clock chimed musically in the hallway, we were feeling our way on tiptoes down the pantry stairs and into the damp, gloomy basement.'

Coils of pungent tobacco spread upwards from Holmes' pipe as he brooded over his next words.

'At first I imagined that a cat or dog might have urinated upon the clay floor, but I quickly realised that the acrid smell was caused by an ammonia leak from one of the four large refrigerators spanning the walls. I made my way over to the first one and with some difficulty, lifted up the lid. Although I had my suspicions as to the contents, it was still quite a shock to me, and poor Wiggins almost collapsed beside me.'

'What was in it?' I demanded.

'Body parts, Watson,' replied Holmes. 'Human body parts. Legs, arms, torsos, cuts of flesh, genitals, hearts, livers, kidneys, brains, coils of intestines, a full head or two. Fortunately, the other three held normal meats that you or I might consume.'

'What do you mean? Real human beings?' I gasped.

'Yes, Watson. Real human remains, packed in ice and kept fresh within the fridge. Mainly female, as far as I could tell. One still had a full head of frozen hair. Where they came from, nobody knows. London is a big city, and people go missing all the time. I have to admit, old man, that Wiggins and I were at sixes and sevens as to what to do next. I rather think he wanted to cut and run. I even thought about it myself. Then we heard a slight creak upon the stairs, switched off the flashlight and withdrew into the gaps between the refrigerators. I had hoped that we might bump into Colonel Alexander Fitzwilton, retired cocoa plantation owner and until recently, Lieutenant-Governor of British New Guinea. Just not at that precise moment.'

'Oh, God. What happened next?' I asked.

'Your new best friend Cynthiah, with two *aitches*, entered the basement like a ghostlike wraith, dressed only in a transparent silk white nightdress, and strolled nonchalantly over to the first freezer. She lifted up the lid, removed a fat, juicy ear and began to suck delicately upon it.'

I sat up abruptly.

'What do you mean, Holmes. A human ear? Sucking! Surely not! That sweet child!' Transparent?

'Not so sweet after all. Really, Watson. Any pretty woman will turn your head. It was apparent to me, if not to poor old Wiggins, that the child was sleepwalking, and not in full control of her actions. I recognised her blank, glassy expression from a previous case. It was before your time, and has not yet been chronicled by your good self.'

I leaned forward on the breakfast table and placed my head in my hands, struggling to concentrate on the facts of this appalling case.

'Even so, Holmes. Even so. She *knew* where these human remains were stored. So she must be a ... a *cannibal* when she is awake as well.'

'I fancy that you might be correct in this, old fellow. It does seem logical. Shall I continue?'

'Oh, yes. Of course.'

'Signalling to Wiggins to keep silent and remain in the basement, and readying my life preserver in my grip, I followed her upstairs.'

'Upstairs? To her bedroom?' I cried.

'Yes, Watson. Into her bedroom,' he replied, with the faintest trace of a smile upon his face.

'Into her bedroom? Where she sleeps? Holmes, you utter swine!'

'Do not worry, old friend. I was not about to take advantage of the young lady. And I'm fairly certain that any propositions on my part would have led to nothing anyway, due to my findings.'

'And what in God's name do you mean by *that* statement?' I almost shrieked.

'Well, do you remember our conversations of last year, about "the love that dare not speak its name?" '

'Oh, sweet Jesus, not that again!' I replied. 'Yes, yes, I recall the musical murders, that included your poor brother and father. Several murders of musical men, by a pair of musical lunatics.'

Holmes scraped away at his pipe, dropping its detritus onto his unfinished bacon and eggs.

'And did I not mention the idea, in the context of the Bloomsbury Group, of musical women?' he enquired.

'Yes. I'm just not ... quite sure what that means.'

'Strange as it may seem, Watson, there are some people for whom sexual pleasure is an end in itself. It means that two women can love one another in the physical sense, in exactly the same way that a man and a woman, or two men, can love each other. For pleasure alone.'

'But how, Holmes? How? That's what puzzles me.'

'Oh, in a variety of ways, I suspect. Kissing and hugging, and all that intimate stuff.'

'And exactly how do you know this?' I enquired.

'As well as finding the harem disguise within her wardrobe, complete with a built-in bustle to make her look fatter, and the purple beaded taffeta dress that she bought as a present for Maureen, I found this, hidden inside a drawer.'

He handed me a photograph, like a magician producing a rabbit out of a hat. I looked at it once and flung it back at him in disgust.

'Holmes, this is too much! It is a picture of two naked women, in each other's arms, and they are kissing!' I protested, pointing at it.

'Indeed it is, old chap. And not just any two naked women. It is a photo of Cynthiah Fitzwilton and Maureen O'Reilly, taken with one of those modern Leica delayed-action cameras, and presumably before the latter was cut up.'

I grabbed it again and forced myself to examine the features of both women.

'Good God! It most certainly is the same poor girl as in that photo in her little room in Royal Crescent. And Cynthiah. This would seem to support your theory that these two young women were ... doing things to each other?'

'I believe so, Watson. I couldn't have put it more pawkily myself. Remember when Lily said her friend would try anything once? Perhaps this was an experiment for her, which went badly wrong, ending in her death, and subsequent harvesting.'

'Harvesting? That is such a cruel word, Holmes! Anyway we must ensure that Lily does not see that,' I muttered sadly, handing him back his picture. 'Well? Was that the conclusion of your nocturnal escapade?'

'Yes. Wiggins and I left the way we had entered, without any fuss.'

'Thank heavens for that. And at least we have established a connection between the two women,' I mused. 'But there are too many unanswered questions in this case for my liking. For instance, why was she dumped into the sewer, rather than chopped up like all the others? And why do these horrible crimes have to keep

110

happening to us in our later years, when we should be taking it easy?'

Holmes leapt up from the table and buttoned his jacket.

'The last question is the easiest to answer. Good old Pottyrot and Wimpsey would not touch them with a proverbial barge-pole. And we are about to discover the answer to your other question. Lestrade is due to meet us outside number 40 Norland Square at eleven bells, where the ferret-faced ingenue will be questioning the bumptious New Guinea Colonel and his errant daughter on the subject of frozen body parts and Maureen O'Reilly's murder. Her autopsy was carried out first thing this morning, and it proved that the poor maid died from strangulation, prior to having her buttocks and thigh torn open, and her eyes removed. Strangely enough, eating someone else is not yet a crime in this country, provided the individual died naturally. Neither can two musical women be prosecuted for making love, in accordance with the ancient Greek cult of Sappho, from the island of Lesbos. Unlike two musical men, which is rather unfair. Hurry up, old fellow. You are about to meet the adorable Cynthiah, with two *aitches*, once again. By the way, did you know that her name is an anagram of hyacinth?'

Cynthiah? Hyacinth? Sappho? Leswho?

A determined Jasper Lestrade was pacing up and down Norland Square in the mizzling rain when our growler pulled in at number 40. In the cab Holmes confirmed that his first inclination as to the relationship between the two girls had been the flowers in Maureen's room. He also hinted at a darker element in their love affair, but would not expand upon the subject until he had talked to Cynthiah herself and 'had all of the facts at his fingertips'. For myself, I could not imagine anything darker than cannibalism and two women doing intimate things to each other for mere sexual gratification.

'Are your men posted to the rear, as I suggested?' queried Holmes.

'Yes, Mr. Holmes. And we are also covered at the front. You are sure that you know what is going on?' asked Lestrade.

'Yes,' replied Holmes grimly. I could see his hand gripping the leather cudgel in his pocket. As usual, he was ready for the worst.

'Shall we begin?'

At a nod from Holmes, Lestrade slammed the lion's head knocker rapidly three times upon the door. I have to admit that, even though my leg had begun to throb with the change of weather, I was looking forward to the reaction of Cynthiah and her bullying father to our reappearance in normal clothes, flies firmly buttoned up and *sans* disguise. Beggars, indeed!

The door was opened cautiously by Colonel Alexander Fitzwilton himself. He was wearing an ill-fitting royal blue dressing gown over glaring tartan pyjamas, with scuffed brown sandals. His left hand flicked away at a half-smoked cigar.

'Yes? What is it?' He grunted.

'The police. Scotland Yard,' replied Lestrade, a trifle too aggressively, I thought. 'I am Detective Lestrade and this is Sherlock Holmes and Dr. Watson. May we come in? We would like to talk to you about a missing girl.'

'And to your daughter, of course,' added Holmes.

'I see. Well. Cynthiah is out at the moment, attending Morning Service,' answered the Colonel, impassively.

'She sings in the choir at St. John The Baptist Church, but will be back shortly. Please. Come in, gentlemen.'

He waved us into the hall and thence through a door into a replica of the Carstairs' front drawing-room.

'No, thank you,' replied Lestrade to the proferred seats. Holmes also shook his head, while I sat down thankfully opposite Fitzwilton.

'The girl's name was Maureen O'Reilly, and we believe that she was strangled,' said Lestrade. When he received no reaction, he continued, 'Her body was dumped into the sewer system outside your house, and washed up yesterday at Abbey Mills.'

Colonel Fitzwilton gazed at Holmes and myself through narrowed eyes, smoke curling from his lips, as though struggling to remember where he had seen us before. Holmes, ever the showman, dropped into his Scottish beggar persona, legs akimbo, stretched out his hand, and pleaded 'Och, surrrr. Cain ye no' spear a wee shillun' fur pooer browken Bruce?'

Lestrade frowned at this improvised bravado, but Fitzwilton's face turned a dark shade of purple. He flung his cigar into the grate angrily.

'All right. So you two clowns masqueraded as beggars to get into my house and abuse my daughter's kindness and hospitality. I don't see why you should be so very proud of such a charade.'

Holmes straightened up and replied calmly in his normal voice.

'Maureen O'Reilly was an innocent, uneducated servant, who was seduced by your evil daughter into a sexual relationship that involved some very dangerous fantasies, one of which led to her death. A death that I suspect was accidental.'

113

'Accidental?' chimed Lestrade and myself in harmony.

Before the boorish Australian could react, Holmes produced a page of scrunched-up newspaper from his pocket and handed it to Lestrade, pointing to a particular section.

'This is where his daughter, Cynthiah Fitzwilton, advertised in the Evening Standard for a *vore*, otherwise known as a *vorarephile*. Notice that she used a popular camouflage, whereby the word *vore* is replaced by the more common anagram *rove*.'

'Holmes,' I protested, 'That all sounds completely foreign to me and utterly disgusting. What in our dear Lord's name is a *vor-ar-e-phile*?'

'He, or she, is someone who wishes to be eaten by another, Watson. To be a cannibal's victim. I suspect that Maureen O'Reilly did not understand what it meant either, but answered it anyway, being of an adventurous nature. It is usually just a sexual fantasy, but it seems to have gotten a little out of hand in this case. Am I not right, Fitzwilton?'

The Colonel sank back into the sofa, holding his head in his hands. The brash exterior began to evaporate before our eyes. His shoulders slumped and he heaved an enormous sigh, almost of relief, as though he had come to an important decision. Then he shrugged his shoulders in resignation, withdrew his hands, puffed out his cheeks and began to speak.

'Gentlemen. Cynthiah ... Cynthiah is *not* evil. Innocent is a more accurate word. Neither is she my natural daughter. In fact, I have never been married. I *rescued* her from a cannibal tribe called the Dobraduras in British New Guinea when she was fifteen. They had captured her as a little baby from a touring English family, whom they

114

ate. Their chief took a liking to the innocent white child, and raised her as his own, teaching her all of the uncivilised practices of that tribe, which I shall not go into here. Suffice it to say that I adopted her formally, and took it upon myself to rid her of those appalling habits, some of which pertained to the kind of games that you mentioned, Mr. Holmes. My housekeeper and I educated her ourselves for a few years, and she went to a finishing school in Brisbane when she reached eighteen.'

He paused to remove a fresh cigar from a flask in his dressing-gown. Both hands shook slightly as he bit off the end and spat it into the fireplace. Then he licked the tip and put a match to it.

'By and large, her education was a success, with one unfortunate exception, which was her taste in human flesh. Because of her childhood in the jungle, she saw ... sees ... nothing wrong with eating other human beings. I have not been able to persuade her otherwise. I was prepared to accept her liking for her own sex as part of her nature and upbringing. It did not trouble me, unlike the cannibalism. With the Dobraduras, as soon as a female child reaches the age of twelve, she is given to an older woman to be initiated into what we would call homosexual love-making. It is a strange tribe, with almost total separation of the sexes, and the women holding dominance over the men. It was their initial criticism of the male hunters' pathetic haul of pigs and chickens that caused the men to start invading other tribes for human meat.'

'God in Heaven!' I spluttered. 'How obscene!'

'Quiet, Watson,' ordered Holmes. 'Continue, Colonel.'

Cynthiah's father leaned forward on the sofa and drew upon his cigar, blowing a thin cloud of smoke from the corner of his mouth.

'Several months ago, when I retired from my position as Lieutenant-Governor of New Guinea, I decided to relocate the pair of us to a more civilised country, where I felt that the prevailing mores might have some influence upon her aberrant tastes. Then having bought this house, I knew that I would have to bring certain ... remains with me from that benighted country, in order to feed her when she succumbed to temptation. I could not allow her to go looking for it in the streets or graveyards of London, as she is in the habit of sleep-walking.'

'Hence the freezer in the basement,' said Holmes.

'What? How do ...?

'Never mind that now,' interrupted Holmes. 'Where did you get these unfortunate souls?'

'I did not kill them, if that's what you mean! It was all done perfectly legally. Otherwise I would not have been able to transport the freezer by ship without being discovered. They were people who had volunteered their bodies to medical science in British New Guinea. I am a qualified doctor, and practised as a surgeon before joining the government over there. It was simple enough to arrange. Although you might argue that medical science was not strictly the purpose of the exercise.'

'Hah! That is most certainly the understatement of the year!' I cried.

At that moment a door banged shut in the hall. Moments later, Cynthiah Fitzwilton appeared in the doorway, looking in surprise at the three strangers in the drawing-room.

'Papa! You did not tell me that you were expecting guests for Sunday lunch,' she remonstrated.

Her father stood up and grasped her hands tenderly in his.

'Cynthiah. These men are not here to eat with us. They have come about your flapper friend, Maureen O'Reilly. We must be honest with them, regardless of the consequences, and tell them the true story of what happened. If necessary, I can call upon the best lawyers in London. Everything will be alright. Trust me. Please sit down over here.'

'Perhaps you might care to explain Maureen's death to us, Miss Fitzwilton?' enquired Holmes.

It was clear to me that Cynthiah did not recognise either of us from our disguises, something that was a considerable relief to me now that I was becoming more aware of the young lady's true nature. Perhaps Holmes had been his usual prescient self when he called her evil. But how on earth had he learned about these sex ... games? Sometimes the sheer range of his knowledge was bewildering.

'It was just an accident,' she burst out immediately. 'Maureen had become bored with pretending to be eaten by me, so we started to play a different game called *Tampulma Walmi* that I was taught by my first love-parent many years ago. It is very simple, but can be dangerous. Near to the final stage of love-making, one girl ties a rope around her neck to cut off the supply of oxygen to the brain, thereby enhancing her pleasure. But Maureen had tied her knot too tightly, and she ... suffocated before I could rescue her. I was too busy with my rope and too involved in my own pleasure. That is the truth.'

'So you decided to cut her up anyway, and cook some bits of her?' broke in Lestrade, astonished.

'Of course,' replied Cynthiah innocently. 'Why not? Then I would benefit from her protein, and she would live forever within me. I loved her.'

Colonel Fitwilton placed his hand fondly around his daughter's shoulder and moved her gently over to the sofa.

'It was I who prevented my daughter from completely harvesting Miss O'Reilly,' he said. 'And I also disposed of the body into the sewer a few nights ago. I ... I just wanted to protect her from herself, and the values of this society, which she does not understand.'

'Madness. Pure madness,' I muttered to myself. This case was beyond my comprehension. I found it difficult to contain my feelings in front of these two ... savages. Unlike Holmes, always the sword of reason in any situation.

He stood up, like an executioner before a guillotine.

'It is at the very least a manslaughter charge for your daughter, Fitzwilton, and for you, aiding and abetting that manslaughter. A judge and a jury of your peers will consider the rights and wrongs of your behaviour, even though there are no existing laws against cannibalism and lesbianism in this country. Perhaps as a result of this case, there will be. I most certainly hope so. Watson, I feel the need for some fresh air.'

'Yes, Holmes. So do I.' I stood up abruptly to join him on his way out.

Before leaving the pair to Lestrade and the British justice system, I felt that I could not depart without asking Miss Fitzwilton one simple question.

'Why do you insist upon consuming your fellow mortals, young lady?'

'You have never tasted human flesh, have you, sir?' she replied, smiling sweetly.

5. Sherlock Holmes And The Richmond Werewolf.

'Watson, the needle!'

'No!'

'What do you mean, no? Where the bloody hell is it?'

'I'm not going to tell you! We agreed that you would take a maximum of two dosages a week, and you had one yesterday. You must wait until Thursday for the next one.'

'You fat old ... bastard! Hah! Don't worry. I shall soon find it,' Holmes cackled gleefully, as he ransacked the bookshelves, flinging his indices, dictionaries, files, notebooks and newspaper clippings to the ground in a desperate search for his cocaine stash. Our desks suffered a similar fate, as did his chemistry bench, where he swept the retorts, test tubes, Bunsen burners and other laboratory equipment onto the floor with one grandiose, furious gesture. The contents of the drawers in the dining table followed. For some reason the mantlepiece was spared his euphoria. When he had finished in the sitting-room, he bounded up the stairs like an athletic ape, taking them three at a time towards my room and a continuation of his pathetic foraging.

I remained calmly seated, being somewhat fagged out after a restless night, due to the effect of the extreme July heat upon my Maiwand leg wound. The sports pages of the Times did not serve to improve my mood. England were following on in the third Test at Headingly, the Australian team having notched up almost 500 runs in their first innings. The best that we could hope for now was another wretched draw, providing Hobbs and

Sutcliffe could negotiate Clarrie Grimmett's devious googlies for long enough.

Holmes had experienced considerable difficulty in withdrawing from the triple dose he had self-administered during the horrible affair of the Holland Park cannibal several months earlier, a case that had resulted in the swift deportation of Colonel Alexander Fitzwilton and his human-eating daughter, Cynthiah, back to British New Guinea. I should have guessed from his mania that he had found my first hiding place within the base of the gramophone player. But I was confident that he would not repeat his success this time. Lily Hudson, our vivacious cockney housekeeper, had agreed to secrete his box of tricks in her 'slave quarters' on the ground floor. Even I did not know where it was kept.

Holmes reappeared at the door, wild-eyed and frantic.

'I could do without a solution next week?' he pleaded. 'I promise. Oh, please, Watson!'

'No.'

His eyes narrowed and his features took on a look of ferocious cunning, like a cat hunting a finch.

'I know you, Watson. All I need do is put myself in your place, slow down my brain considerably and think in your customary dull manner. That way I shall discover where it is.'

I ignored this insult while he sat down opposite me on the basket-chair and stared at me with his piercing eyes, fingers steepled below his nostrils. I glared back at him, stony-faced, like his new hero, Buster Keaton. Holmes' pupils were huge black dilations against thin grey fringes.

'You need to be taken out of yourself, my dear chap,' I suggested. 'It is such a glorious day. I have been invited to a garden party out in Richmond, to celebrate the tenth anniversary of the role of the Northumberland Fusiliers in the Battle Of The Somme. Why not join me as my guest? We could take a cab and then a short stroll along the Thames to Ham House. Some sunshine will do us both good. Anyway, I shall go alone if you do not wish to come. I am looking forward to seeing my old comrades again.'

He ignored my words and continued to gawk at me. I refused to prolong his psychotic little game and returned to my newspaper and to keeping a watchful eye on the German economy. This was a small hobby of mine since the disastrous Versailles Treaty, which agreed a cost of reparations for the Great War that I felt to be rather unfair on the German people. Yet the country's recent entry into the League Of Nations seemed a hopeful sign. The article was a dull read, but at least I had corned brisket beef with white cabbage fried in butter and bouillon potatoes to look forward to at lunch, according to Lily.

Needless to say, it did not take the great detective very long to penetrate my mind.

'Downstairs! That's it, isn't it? Lily has it! Watson, that is *exactly* the type of boring thing you would do! Remove the temptation from our rooms altogether! MISS HUDSON! MISS HUDSON! Here. Perhaps I'll ring her precious gong for her. She'll come soon enough then.'

Holmes danced over to the fireplace and banged his fist several times harshly into the bell that Lily had installed specifically to prevent him from screaming her name down the stairs whenever he wanted her. Almost immediately I heard the clump, clump, clump of her clodhoppers on the stairs, and her concomitant grumbling slang.

'ere, ere, Mr 'Olmes. Yer dahn't need tah smash thah bleedin' thin'. Wot 'ja wan', ainyways? Oi've go' a dish in thah oven wot needs watchin'.'

'I want my needle and my medicine, Miss Hudson, and I want them now,' Holmes commanded imperiously.

Lily looked over at me. I shook my head.

'Nah,' she replied. 'Watsey sez nah, an' tha's good 'nuff fer me. Bye.'

'What?' screamed Holmes. 'You will take orders from this ... this ... mere ... *subordinate*, but not from me?'

His paranoia was evident as he stepped in front of our housekeeper and tried to prevent her leaving by spreading out his arms and legs to provide a barrier. Lily made to kick him with one of her boots. I lay down my paper wearily. With cocaine addiction, anything can happen, and probably would. He might even damage himself. Giving him a dose was fast becoming the lesser of two evils.

'Holmes, if we give you a *four*-per-cent solution, will you take my advice, and join me for the garden party in Surrey this afternoon?'

'Oh, yes, Watson, yes. Anything! ANYTHING!'

It was well after three o'clock by my fob watch when we stepped down from our carriage at the end of Nightingale Lane in Richmond, just a short stroll from the Thames. In comparison to his morning behaviour, Holmes appeared subdued. He did not seem like his normal self after a cocaine injection, which usually induced a degree of facetious merriment and continuous ribbing of yours truly. Our conversation had been entirely one-sided on the trip, his interest in cricket being slender at the best, and as we fell into step along the deserted tow path, I decided to follow his example and enjoy the blazing July sunshine in comradely silence as we headed towards Ham House and Eel Pie Island. It was so warm that I was forced to loosen my old blue and beige regimental tie, an unusual event for me in an English summer. That was when I first noticed the six mute swans.

They were running along the surface of the river, in that inimitable fashion they have, webbed feet slapping along the water while their wings flapped in desperation, as though they were preparing to take off on a long flight, but couldn't quite manage it. I was enjoying the rhythm of their sounds so much that I failed to notice the tune that Holmes was tapping out on his fingers in full musical harmony with the swans.

'Di-di-dit, dah-dah-dah, di-di-dit, di-di-dit, dah-dah-dah, di-di-dit. Are you familiar with Morse code, Watson?' he asked.

'Holmes. What a question for an ex-military man! Of course!'

'So you recognise the message they are sending us?'

'No. There is no message, Holmes,' I sighed. 'They are simply swans struggling to gain flight.'

'It is "S.O.S., S.O.S." They are using the international distress signal. We must help them.'

'Holmes, that is entirely your imagination speaking. And your drug habit. Which I am frankly getting very fed up with!'

'Don't look behind you, old fellow, but we are being followed.'

'You really are paranoid, you know that? Hallucination is one of the side effects of cocaine. I believe I will hand control of your dosage back to your good self from now on,' I exclaimed hotly. 'And start looking for new digs.'

Nevertheless I could not prevent myself from casting a backward glance over my shoulder. Sure enough a middle-aged man was strolling about twenty yards behind. He was a clean-shaven, foppish dandy in a dark blue suit, who sported a huge mane of unruly red hair. His lips were parted in laughter at some private joke and he swung his cane as though he had not a care in the world.

Holmes stopped abruptly, and pretended to examine with great interest some wild celandine that sprang from a bush at the side of the path. I noticed our friend also came to a halt, and had bent down to tie his shoelace. Holmes was right!

'Sorry about that Morse code business, Watson. Just wanted to grab your attention. You seemed a trifle withdrawn. Does he remind you of anyone? Someone from our distant past? A past that involved water? A mountain in Switzerland? Fighting? Falling?'

'Me? Withdrawn? Hah! What a joke *that* is!' I muttered, bending over to examine the wild flowers. Exasperated, it took me a little while to realise what Holmes was suggesting.

'You don't mean ...?'

'Precisely,' he murmured to the bright yellow perennials. 'Moriarty himself. The Napoleon of crime. He could be a relation, with the same criminal strain in his blood. Identical height, protruding forehead, willowy frame and rolling gait. Although unmarried, the Professor did have a younger brother, I seem to remember. A station master in the west of England, was he not?'

'A Colonel James Moriarty. Who could very well have had a son,' I muttered back to the celandines.

'Intent on some form of vengeance?' suggested the reborn flowerlover.

'Served very cold indeed. Perhaps we should confront the damned popinjay?' I suggested to the bush.

'No. We can handle him, I am sure, between us. I happen to have brought my persuader with me. Let us continue our walk, but keep our eyes peeled for any friends he might have invited along.'

Holmes stood up and we continued our leisurely ramble. I gripped my cane more firmly, in case it needed swift transformation into a weapon.

'I must apologise for my behaviour this morning, Watson. I don't know what came over me. Most unlike my true, unemotional self, I'm sure you agree.'

'Apology accepted,' I replied breezily, enlivened at the prospect of danger. 'It is clearly to do with your return to the use of cocaine on an irregular basis. Either you stop taking it altogether, or we should agree to a more consistent pattern to your injections. Say, a four-per-cent solution once a day?'

'I believe that I will attempt the former, rather than succumb to the latter, old chap. It is impossible to enjoy life while dependent upon the filthy drug. For instance, just look at those swans again! Are they not beautiful?'

Holmes pointed to the same six stately creatures, disturbing the reflected sky as they drifted nonchalantly in one, two, three formation on the far side of the glassy river. They had obviously decided to stay on the water for the time being, enticed by the prospect of some stale bread from a hefty-looking nurse and her ancient patient in his wheelchair, who were both feeding them liberally.

126

'I have looked upon those brilliant creatures,
And now my heart is sore.
All's changed since I, hearing at twilight,
The first time on this shore,
The bell-beat of their wings above my head,
Trod with a lighter tread.

Yeats was writing about old age, Watson, in his poem, *'The Wild Swans Of Coole'*. He was fifty then, and deeply concerned about his fading powers and the prospect of his own mortality. The swans will live on after his death, and that made him melancholy. Yet over the last ten years he has composed some of his best poetry.'

'Really?'

My friend's new-found interest in literature and the Irish poet Yeats was one of the more puzzling alterations in his character during his time as an apiarist on the Sussex Downs. I feared that I would never quite get used to it, preferring a good adventure story myself, with lots of blood and thunder.

'Is our shadow still on the trail?' he continued, as we moved on.

I glanced behind me, only to find the path empty of anyone.

'No. He seems to have vanished,' I replied.

We had almost reached Hammerton's ferry near Ham House when Holmes stopped suddenly in his tracks and stared wide-eyed at the wheelchair-bound man and his minder, who had kept pace with us, and were now boarding the boat to come across.

'Great God in Heaven!' grunted Holmes. 'Surely it cannot be! He fell onto the rock and was killed, Watson. Did he not? Into the abyss? I saw him fall! I heard that ... sound!'

'Who? What rock? What sound?'

'Why, the Professor, of course,' he breathed, clutching the cane to his chest uneasily. 'The Falls of Reichenbach. His head smashing against the stone above the roar of the torrent, before his body bounced off it and down the river. But look! See the way it moves from side to side in that nervous, reptilian way of his? The head is oscillating! Like a python eyeing its next week's food! Could anyone else have such a disgusting habit?'

My thoughts immediately returned to my friend's cocaine problem and his troubled memories of that dreadful term of trial in 1891. It was not the final problem that I thought it would be, but it had definitely been the end of the Napoleon of crime. Nobody could have survived that fall. No human being, that is. As usual, my friend seemed to read my mind without even looking at me.

'It is not the drug, Watson, I can assure you. See, he is coming towards us! It is surely him! The malignant spider has come back from the dead!'

As the ferry approached us, and Holmes shrank back in disbelief, I realised that even if it was, by some strange stroke of fate, Professor Moriarty, he could hardly pose a threat to us now. Having only seen him in the distance on a couple of occasions, I had never actually met Holmes' arch-foe face to face, and so would not be able to recognise him. This poor soul was very old indeed, and almost certainly paralysed from the waist down and so locked forever into his leather wheelchair. He might even be suffering from Parkinson's Disease, as he seemed to have little control over his head movements. Nevertheless I positioned myself between my colleague and the boat as it came in to berth.

But we had both forgotten about the dandy.

'Please do not turn around. Actually, do not move at all. Unless you wish a bullet or two to pierce your aging flesh.' The brisk voice simulated some tough cowboy accent from across the Atlantic, yet struggled to hide a reedy, feminine undertone at the same time.

'Drop the sticks and place your hands at the back of your necks.'

We obeyed, and waited while the nurse pushed the wheelchair onto the path in front of us. Her patient shuddered and gripped the handles of his mobile chair with gnarled splotchy fingers as he was pushed over a pair of rickety planks onto the edge of the tow-path. Then he blinked up at us from beneath hooded eyes, that held a malignant cruelty within their depths.

'Good afternoon, gentlemen. Verily my cup runneth over. When I sent the good doctor an invitation to a mythical garden party, one that I knew he could not refuse, I half-hoped he might bring along his old colleague as a guest, but did not really expect such a mundane affair to be of interest to the world's *very* first consulting detective.'

The vicious half-whisper was barely audible, the thin, humourless smile scarcely visible on his skeletal features.

'Oh, yes, Mr. Sherlock Holmes. It is indeed I. My, you *do* look well. It would seem that the last thirty-five years have been rather kinder to you than to me.'

He paused, the better to control a coughing fit which concluded in a deathly throat rattle that reminded me of past patients who had been near their end.

'You broke my spine in several places at Reichenbach and scarred my face down the right side forever into this horseshoe wheal. But nevertheless your old nemesis is still alive. Imagine that! Alive, if not exactly kicking! Hah!'

He removed his black opera hat to reveal a shining domed pate and that hideous scar, which looped between chin and forehead. There was a thin beige brace around his neck, presumably also broken in the fall, and therefore responsible for his paraplegic status. A dark frock coat completed his visible attire, which resembled that of a crippled priest.

'But how ...?'

'How did I survive the fall, Dr. Watson?' The voice had risen slightly above a whisper into a phlegmy chuckle. 'By the good fortune of being spotted floating down the river by a pair of youthful American tourists, walking in the mountains. One of the Yankees dived in and pulled my body, scarcely alive, onto the bank. After that? Oh, the rescue, the ambulance, the hospital, the two years of recovery, this damned ... contraption. Permanent disability. All far too boring to spend any time on. Please, Jem, do permit the two gentlemen to lower their hands. I would not want them to be uncomfortable in any way. Not yet, anyway.'

We obliged the Professor gratefully. I noticed that my colleague placed one hand casually into his pocket.

'Nevertheless, be assured that if either of you interfering busybodies make the slightest trouble for me now, Jem will shoot you both without hesitation. He has my instructions.'

Moriarty shifted awkwardly in his chair, his head see-sawing around.

'Half a lifetime ago, you came up against me, and succeeded in destroying my organisation, the product of countless years of work.'

His seething bile was now directed at Holmes alone.

'It has taken me almost thirty difficult years in Germany and the Weimar Republic to recreate a similar syndicate, one that has spread successfully throughout Europe. Now I have returned to England in order to restore my empire here. And what do I find? That the famous bee-keeper of your chronicler's inflated fantasies is also back to detecting! And that he has seriously inconvenienced me yet again on at least one occasion! The lucrative child-trafficking operation that I controlled through the Macaroni family was brought to an end by your meddling interference, Holmes. This time I really cannot afford to let you live. Nor your loyal aide-de-camp, I'm afraid. The situation for you both is utterly impossible.'

The manner in which this wraithlike gargoyle spat out the word 'aide-de-camp' made the blood boil within my veins. I sensed that Holmes was about to pounce upon the crippled Professor and finish off the job he had evidently failed to achieve in Switzerland. I was ready to take on the nancy boy behind when the first move was made, and even for a bullet if necessary, when another gun appeared magically at the end of the nurse's arm.

'Permit me to introduce my nephew and bodyguard Jem and his German wife, Fraulein Hetta,' Moriarty hissed. 'She speaks very little English, but is quite adept with a Luger. As, indeed, am I.'

Another German pistol materialized from beneath the blanket covering the cripple's legs, gripped in a talonous hand.

'I suggest that you both calm down and follow me, if you please. Jem?'

'Move,' said the dandy, pushing his gun roughly into Holmes' back. Normally my colleague would have disarmed Moriarty's nephew quite easily with a simple bartitsu swivel, but instead he removed his hand from his pocket and walked calmly towards the ferry boat. I followed him reluctantly.

'To my ait, Kurt,' ordered Moriarty coldly, when the crippled criminal had been settled once again upon the boat deck.

With not a single soul in sight, the boat phut-phutted its way across to Eel Pie Island, the youthful blonde-haired boatee with the startling blue eyes being also in the Professor's employ. I felt like jumping up and shouting for help, or even diving into the water and risking that bullet, but was held back by Holmes' obvious scrutiny of Moriarty. His previous fear seemed to have dissipated and been replaced by an icy stillness, as he stared gimlet-eyed at the twisted frame within that wheelchair prison, its head swaying gently about. It was the Holmes of old, ready for this final challenge that had appeared from nowhere. He told me once that getting rid of Moriarty's criminal empire was the supreme achievement of his working life, and now the villain was back, albeit crippled! Resurrected, almost! What agonies must he feel?

The engine was switched off and the boat glided for several minutes up a narrow, murky canal to dock eventually at the rear of a half-demolished, half-derelict Palladian villa, which I recognised with surprise as Orleans House, once a famous venue for intemperate parties involving many of Great Britain's leading socialites, including the King and Queen of England themselves.

'Out', chortled the dandy, shoving Holmes and myself forward off the boat. We complied, as all three guns were still trained upon our bodies.

The inside of the octagonal remains of the lichen-covered villa proved to be even more of a ruin. Some of the lower windows had been blocked up completely with wooden boards and there was little light. Cobwebs dripped from the ceiling like fishing nets hanging out to dry. Faded wallpaper peeled from blotched walls. A filthy rug stretched the length of the dust-filled room, which contained no single item of furniture. I stiffened, feeling that it might be the perfect location for a double murder. Yet Holmes seemed quite relaxed, keeping his deadly gaze upon Moriarty.

'Do not worry, Dr. Watson,' whispered the Professor. 'I wish to acquaint Mr. Sherlock Holmes fully with my new operation, so that he can go to his grave knowing the perilous future for his wonderful country. The country that failed to recognise my genius. It will be my vengeance. Take them to the Otis, Jem.'

'You are right about one thing, Professor,' said Holmes equally quietly. 'Any peril that comes to Great Britain will surely be over my dead body.'

'And mine!' I echoed.

'Oh, shut up! Such heroes! Over there! The pair of you!' The dandy waved his Luger around like a flag at a carnival. Holmes touched my arm gently, knowing full well that I was about to risk all by attacking the insufferable clown.

A heavy iron door lay hidden behind a purple drape to the left of the entrance. It led directly onto a dilapidated wooden platform which was just about wide enough to house all five of us, including the grim, bulky frame of Hetta Moriarty, lodged firmly behind the wheelchair, her Luger still pointing at my stomach. Only then did I realise that she was not fat, but heavily pregnant. Another generation of Moriartys! It did not bear thinking about.

'Down', nodded the Professor to his nephew, who must have pressed some unseen button as the floor beneath us shuddered and started to shunter downwards.

'You must understand, Holmes,' wheezed Moriarty. 'That I have purchased the entire island as my headquarters whilst I extend my business from Europe into Britain. After the unfortunate demise of Colonel Sebastian Moran – oh yes, he really *is* dead, natural causes in prison, I believe – my family rallied around me to become my support mechanism. And you are about to meet some more members of that extended family.'

Holmes remained passive and appeared to have little interest in the Professor's words. When the ancient lift vibrated eventually to a halt, we found ourselves inside a dimly-lit wine cellar. The younger Moriarty gestured with his Luger for us to follow him down a corridor of empty wine racks towards a black mahogany door, which he opened onto an ear-piercing, cacophonous racket.

We had entered a factory of some sort, hidden safely within the bowels of Eel Pie Island, and dedicated, I was sure, to the manufacture of dangerous and illegal substances that would enhance Moriarty's criminal empire. There were four lines of ten machine operators, all clones of Kurt the boatman, with their khaki shirts, navy shorts and identical blonde hair. And all with plain white masks as protection from the foetid adour that assaulted our nostrils. Most of them looked like Boy Scouts, still in their teenage years. At school even!

'Welcome, gentlemen,' cackled Moriarty, 'Welcome to my *Wolfsschanze*, my Wolf's Lair.'

'The precise translation of that word would be Wolf's Sconce, would it not?' suggested my colleague innocently.

'Mr. Holmes,' the Professor snarled. 'Your erudition knows no bounds. A knowledge of German syntax should be useful to you in your attempts to comprehend the sheer breadth of my ambition. Which I shall explain to you later, as I need to rest now. Hans! Fritz! Help Jem and Hetta to take these two through to the dungeon. Once there, tie them up securely. Any hint of trouble, shoot them both in each knee.'

Again there was no sign of resistance from Holmes as a pair of tall youths left their positions, grabbed us from behind and frog-marched us out of the bright factory, down several steps, along a narrow corridor and into what looked to me like a vast medieval torture chamber, complete with iron maiden, ancient garrotte and inquisitional chair.

'Holmes!' I cried, desperate for any sign of resistance from my friend as our arms and legs were being trussed up with twisted fishing ropes.

'Let them be about their business, Watson,' he replied calmly. 'We would not wish to give young Moriarty and his gestating hausfrau an excuse to make cripples of us, would we?'

'I can wait, if you can,' grinned the Professor's nephew. 'Tie their hands behind their backs, Hans. And also strap them to each other, back to back. That's it. Two such *dear* friends won't mind a little discomfort. For a night or two anyway.'

Once we had been well and truly chained together on the clay floor, our four jailers departed the dank cell, bolting and locking the iron door behind them. We were plunged into the blackest darkness and forced to shift our bodies around until some semblance of tolerable discomfort was reached. To cap it all, my leg had started to give me gyp.

'I must apologise, Holmes, for getting you into this unholy mess,' I groaned. My voice echoed eerily around the chamber.

'Do not worry, old fellow,' he responded. 'I would not have missed it for anything. A chance to do battle with Moriarty again? Manna from heaven. We must find out what the wizened old villain is up to. And then stop him. The future of our country may depend upon it. However, the odds are not good. We may not make it ourselves. Are you ready for such a conclusion?'

'You know I am.'

'Then let us to work. It is fortunate that I have trained myself to see in the dark. Our friend the nephew has done us a good turn by indicating how long we may be stuck here. Getting rid of these fetters may take a little time. It has been many years since I trained a young man called Harry Houdini in the subtle art of escapology.'

'When was that? You never mentioned it before.'

'Watson, there are several things that you and your benighted readers do not know about my life. One of them happens to be that I am an accomplished magician, illusionist and escape artist. I believe I may have written a trifling monologue on the subject many years ago. Now. Being Sea Scouts, those boys will be familiar with many different knots. I happened to notice how they tied us together, quite carelessly, using one of the simplest of knots to unhitch. It is called a Sheepshank, sometimes referred to as a 'Tom fool' knot. This is where your rotundity and my lack of same will come in useful. Breathe in as deeply as you can and hold it for as long as possible. I shall do that also. Needless to say, I stretched out my stomach to its absolute limit when they were busy tying us up. Did you?'

'Oh, Holmes, it never occurred to me to do such a thing,' I sighed.

I followed my friend's instructions to the best of my ability. Then he started to jiggle his body up and down, bouncing his buttocks on and off the ground like a baby leaning to crawl. This had the effect of causing me to expel air suddenly.

'Sorry,' I said. 'You should have warned me.'

'Never mind. Let us try it again.'

We bounced up and down together painfully for about ten minutes, until I felt the rope around my body riding loosely at my neck. With one final jounce, it disappeared over my head, and I was able to shunt around and face, I assumed, my old friend and colleague.

'Holmes? Are you there? Are you free?'

'Yes, old chap. That was the easy part. Now we must attack our arms and legs. Turn around again and let me feel the rope around your wrists, now that I can move my hands behind my back.'

I obeyed, and soon felt my friend's fingers groping through mine to my wrists, where they settled upon the rope and traced it several times around my arms.

'Dear me,' he muttered.

'What? Is it difficult?'

'Hhmm. It feels like a Surgeon's Knot, or a variation of same. It is used as a suture for tying ligatures, as I'm sure you know.'

'Of course,' I replied. 'But there are many different kinds.'

After several further minutes of ticklish fingerplay, Holmes muttered, 'I know what this is. A Double-double Granny Knot. They are notoriously difficult to unpick. Now if I can just free your hands ...'

There followed a good hour of fiddling with my ropes, interspersed with frequent colourful oaths from my friend. The great escapologist had to rest his tired fingers several times, and failed to respond to my attempts at conversation, until I finally suggested that we explore alternative methods of freeing ourselves.

'It is really no use, Holmes. This is positively tortuous. We must try something else.'

'Of course! Well done! Good old Watson! You never cease to amaze me. Pure genius! Why did I not think of that? The spiked chair in the corner! We might be able to cut through the ropes with one of the barbs on the foot-rest. *Out of the mouth of babes and sucklings ...*'

'*.... hast thou ordained strength because of thine enemies, that thou mightest still the enemy and the avenger. Psalm 8.*'

'Touché. Now, if I can just stand ... up, maybe I can hop across to it.'

'Do be careful!' I warned. 'Those things might still be sharp!'

'That, my dear chap, is rather the whole point, if you can pardon the pun!' said Holmes, as he hopped across the room. 'Don't worry, Watson. I have no intention of sitting in it. Oh God! Ouch!'

'Are you all right?' I cried.

'Yes, yes. Just bumped straight into the damn thing. I can settle myself on the floor again, like so, and place my back against the inquisitional chair. Did you know, Watson, that these devices were made of iron, which could be heated underneath with coals, just in case the pain from the skewers proved insufficient?'

'No. Thank God we live in a different time.'

'Do we? I have no doubt that Moriarty is planning their reintroduction for our sole benefit, once he has boasted about his dastardly plan to destroy Britain. Oh, excellent. I have discovered a sharpish one right at the end. If I can fray the rope by pulling it backwards and forwards along the tip, like so ...'

For a long while the only sounds in the dungeon were my friend's grunts and groans as he worked the spike across his tied wrists. I remained silent, wondering what we would do if we managed to free ourselves. How could we escape from this infernal chamber of horrors?

'There!' shouted Holmes finally. 'Got it! Now for my legs. Really, it is so much easier to untie a knot when your hands are free. Good. I shall do the same for you.'

Once we were both able to stand up, rubbing our wrists, Holmes asked, 'What now, eh, Watson? First let us check this door to ensure that we are, in fact, inside a genuine locked room mystery. Quietly, if you please. There may be a sentry outside. Have you got your vestas with you?'

Fortunately our pockets had not been examined by our captors, so I was able to shed some light on the prison by striking a match. This caused a brief scuttling from one of the corners.

'Rats,' commented Holmes matter-of-factly. 'And where there are rats, there are rat-holes. Bring the match over to that corner and let us find it.'

If my colleague thought the hole might be of some assistance in our escaping from the prison cell, he was disappointed. It was a tiny two inch gap in the bottom of a wall. We examined the door and the clay floor, all to no avail. Then Holmes started to tap around the walls for a loose stone.

'What about the iron maiden?' I mused, wandering over with a freshly-lit match and turning an old warden lock at the side. With some effort, I hauled open the rusty, squeaking hinge of the sarcophagus.

There was a skeleton inside.

'Holmes!' I cried.

'What is it? Oh, good God, a human being! One of us, eh? Hhmm. Which has been inside this metal trap for a very long time indeed. Calm yourself. You have seen enough of them, I'm sure. This poor chap is *very* dead. About fifty years dead, I'd say. Picked clean by those same rats, coming in through the top. Judging by the state of his broken bones, he was probably beaten up quite badly first. He was a youngish, single man, maybe in his late twenties when he died. The length of his skull and teeth would suggest that he was an Arab from the Middle East. Also this discoloration in his left ankle proves that he was a leper, which might help to explain his mode of passing. His work was of a purely manual nature, possibly in building roads. And he spent a large part of his life in prayer. Note the worn knee bones. Oh, well. His skeleton is of little use in our present dilemma. No, wait! Maybe it is! Watson, grab a finger and break it off. I'll do the same, and we can use them to work open a stone or two on the wall. I believe I may have found a loose one over by the garrotte.'

'Holmes, that is absolute sacrilege! Interfering with his remains! Even if he was an Arab!'

'Would you prefer that someone else play with your own skeleton in fifty years time? And that Moriarty be allowed to bring our beloved country to its knees?'

I was forced to yield to this discouraging prospect, and soon Holmes and I were scraping around a set of worn blocks behind the appalling garrotte with the two forefingers of the aforementioned dead Arab. Despite their great age, both white bones held their strength well as we progressed to the stage of being able to remove two stones from the wall. Looking through them, there was nothing to see but ... mud. Mud and more mud.

'What now?' I asked, somewhat facetiously.

'We continue,' replied Holmes, as he worked on the surrounding stone with his home-made implement. 'How many more matches have you left?'

'About twenty,' I replied.

'It will have to be enough. Unfortunately I left all my smoking equipment at 221B Baker Street. Let us work in the dark for a while. Eh, I may not have mentioned it, Watson, but I do know a little about the history of Eel Pie Island.'

'I could certainly do with a piping hot eel pie right now,' I muttered.

Ignoring my grumbling stomach, Holmes continued. 'Legend has it that Henry VIII was being rowed up the Thames on the Royal Barge one day, and while passing the island, he was overcome by hunger, and said, "Stop the barge and bring me an eel pie!" He sent a minion ashore to buy him one from a stall, acquired a taste for the pies, and then frequently indulged it from then on. This island is naught but a mudbank, Watson. If we can remove enough bricks, we may be able to tunnel through the surrounding mud to our freedom.'

'Or to the river?'

'Perhaps. You can swim, can't you? What time is it now?'

'It is almost 20.00 hours. Seven fifty-eight.'

'Right. Just keep scratching, and save the matches. We may need them later on, if only to set fire to Moriarty's evil factory.'

We continued to scrape and scour for what felt like an eternity to my own poor arthritic fingers, but was in reality only twenty-nine minutes by my watch. That was when Holmes' hand slipped forwards through a hole in about two feet of mud.

'Eureka!' he cried. 'It is merely a mud wall, fronted by stone. What lies beyond, I wonder, eh, Watson?'

I needed no further encouragement to start shifting mud enthusiastically from the wall and onto the floor in great big dollops, until there was enough space for us both to crawl through. But were we free?

'I shall go first, just in case there are any surprises,' said Holmes.

'Here,' I said, handing him the box of vestas. 'Bring the matches and use them to see where you are.'

Holmes climbed through the hole and disappeared from my view. I heard the sound of a match flaring up, followed by a muted '*Yes!*'.

'What is it?' I demanded.

'Freedom, Watson. Maybe. Hurry up.' His voice echoed back to me from the far side of the hole. I sank my fists into the thick slimy mud and swam slowly through, to land painfully on what seemed to be an underground dried-up riverbed, with the merest hint of a trickle of water downwards. This was something I was familiar with from my time in Afghanistan.

'It is a wadi, Holmes,' I said. 'And a very smelly one at that.'

'Perhaps. More of a tunnel, I would say. The chemical odour might be caused by an outflow from Moriarty's factory. Which is where the water may also originate. We must head upwards to find its source. Follow me. I shall light a match every so often.'

We progressed through the underground passage, having to crouch down and land occasional kicks at scuttling rats. I held a handkerchief to my nose to control the effects of the worsening stench, which did not seem to bother my friend. The heat was suffocating, the tunnel was narrowing worryingly, my leg throbbed constantly and I felt that I could not last much longer, when Holmes let out a satisfied sigh.

'Aha! What have we down here?'

'Some sort of drainage pipe,' I replied. It was situated on the bottom right hand side of the tunnel, and was responsible for the chemical waste.

'Which is wide enough for us both to crawl through. My guess is that it will lead up into the factory. Follow me, Watson!'

Inch by inch we crawled through the foul-smelling effluent using our elbows and toes for traction. Fortunately it was only a few minutes before Holmes' legs disappeared from view and I too was able to exit the tube and find myself in a corner drain of the same factory that we had glimpsed earlier in the day. Except this time nobody was working and there were no signs of the Professor's Boy Scouts. All was silent and each workplace was dimly-lit by an eerie overhead fluorescent lamp.

'Now let us discover what particular hell that mighty warped brain has been conjuring up,' whispered Holmes, rubbing his hands together.

'Eh, should we not concentrate on getting off this muddy hell-hole for good, and seeking Lestrade's assistance in destroying the Professor's empire?' I suggested meekly.

'No, Watson. No. We must find out what devilment the old coot is up to. After that, he belongs to me. Regardless of what happens, I will finish him off for good now, as I failed to do once before.'

'But the man is close to his natural end, Holmes,' I murmured. 'He may have only a few months to go. Why not ... leave him be?'

'Never. While Moriarty lives, my life is worthless. All those cases you embellished so colourfully might as well never have happened.'

'But how will we do it without some form of weaponry?'

'We must find a way. First let us examine one of these tables.'

Holmes was in his element as he fingered his way through the various chemical apparatuses, murmuring their names as he went along. To me the array of laboratory equipment seemed identical to his own, back in our Baker Street sitting room. Finally he reached a simple phial half-filled with white powder, unscrewed the cap and tasted its contents.

'I wonder if you can guess what this is, old chap,' he said, smiling.

'Do tell.'

'Your friend and mine. A crystalline tropane alkaloid that is obtained from the leaves of the coca plant. Did you know that chewing coca leaves became widespread throughout South America three thousand years ago, when the plant was believed to be a gift from a generous God? Moriarty is manufacturing the drug cocaine. To a very high standard, I must admit.'

'Cocaine?' I almost shouted. 'Good grief! Holmes! It is no friend of ours. Because its use is now banned in Britain, your unfortunate habit has led to us both becoming in effect, criminals. If Jasper Lestrade knew about it, he would have to arrest us.'

'Sometimes the law can be such an ass, Watson.'

'Perhaps,' I replied. 'But tell me this. If supplies of this awful drug are so readily available, why should manufacturing and producing cocaine bring Great Britain to its knees?'

'You are quite right. There must be more to this than meets the eye. Just another quick sample before we investigate the other work tables.'

It soon became clear to us that the entire room was dedicated solely to the production of cocaine in the form of white powder. In one corner lay many containers of completed phials, and in another the raw material, a veritable cornucopia of copa leaves, piled high to the ceiling. The swine Moriarty must have imported them from South America and brought them up the Thames to Eel Pie Island on a barge.

'What now, Holmes?' I whispered, hoping that the answer might include a swift departure from the island and a safe return to Baker Street and one of Lily's excellent late suppers, washed down by a brandy or three.

'We must find Moriarty and kill him,' he replied grimly. 'That is the only way to bring down his empire. Send him to the dark valley in which all paths meet. Just look over here, Watson.'

He was pointing to another corner of the factory, which contained several layers of cardboard boxes, each of which was labelled with the name of a specific child's sweet. There were jellies, fudges, gums, mints, varieties of chocolates, liquorice and many others.

'Oh, jellies. I adore them,' I said. 'Can I try one?'

'Watson, this is no time for jellies. What do you notice about these sweets? What is their common denominator?'

'Eh, sugar?'

'Yes, but no. Notice they are all *soft*. And this last table contains an array of needles. What if Moriarty is planning to inject cocaine into the centre of these products, and distribute them around the country, in order to create a dependency among the next generation? Their parents will put their erratic behaviour down to sugar, but in fact, it will have been caused by liquid cocaine.'

'Won't they get sick, and stop eating the sweets?'

'That is where his genius comes in. Just a tiny amount might be used, so little that it cannot be noticed by laboratory tests, or the children themselves. They will grow up with a need for the drug – believe me, I know all about this – and cease to be of any use to the country in future conflicts. What if there is another major war then? Those German Boy Scouts will be prepared, right enough, but their English equivalent will not.'

'If it works, it is surely a fiendish plan,' I agreed.

'Be quiet! Quick! Down behind these boxes! Somebody is coming through from the wine cellar!'

More than one body actually entered the factory. Holmes and I pressed ourselves closer to the wall behind the containers. The two newcomers were chatting away in a guttural German dialect, which sounded like nonsense to me, with my limited war patois. I could see that Holmes was straining to understand their words. And that he had placed his hand inside his pocket again.

I peered around the edge of a box to see two pairs of legs – not wearing shorts, so they were not Boy Scouts – heading for the opposite corner of the room. Their words now seemed more familiar to me, and I soon realised that they were counting – *eine*, *zwei*, *drei*, *vier*, etc., – presumably carrying out an inventory of the finished product.

Holmes placed a finger to his lips and indicated for me to remain hidden behind the boxes. He withdrew the persuader from his pocket, held it within the palm of his hand, and stood up. Then he moved swiftly through the worktables across to the pair of stockkeepers, prattling away in fluent German and smiling as he went. I had enough of the language to recognise something about needing a match to light his pipe. They were so surprised that before they could react properly he was upon them and had coshed the taller one with his life preserver. The other was pinned, whining, against the wall.

'Watson! Hurry up! Grab their pistols and keep watch at the cellar door.'

I obeyed instantly, while Holmes started to interrogate the thin, pasty-faced clerk with the silly square black moustache, who had dropped his pencil and clipboard in terror.

'*Wo ist der Professor?*' Holmes lifted his persuader threateningly above the weasel's head.

'*Agh ... er wird in agh ... seinem Hotel ruht,*' he gurgled.

'*Wo ist das Hotel?*'

'*Auf der anderen Seite der Insel.*'

'*Danke.*' With that Holmes slammed his weapon onto the man's head, and joined me by the door.

'Moriarty is resting at his hotel on the other side of the island. Let us go. Hand me one of those Lugers. Are they fully loaded? Excellent.'

And so we made our uninterrupted way back up the lift and out of Orleans House onto the island. It was 9.35 and beginning to get dark when we emerged, our guns firmly in our belts. The fresh air was like a balm to my senses.

'Over here, Watson. There is an obvious path. Be ready for anything.'

'I am. But I still believe that we are too old to become vigilantes. Especially against at least forty-one armed Boy Scouts, as well as the Professor, his nephew and his pregnant wife. How many bullets does one of these Lugers hold?'

'Eight. I know the mathematics does not work out, but nothing will prevent me from finishing him off. He must pay the price, as we all must pay. Are you with me, or against me?'

'With you, of course.'

'Then leave the Professor to me. But you must watch my back. Would you like to sniff some of this first? It will heighten your energy levels.'

My friend handed me one of the phials of cocaine.

'No, thank you, Holmes,' I replied coldly.

'Well, I'll have a quick snort before we go any further. Aaaaaah! Just look at those swans again, rising up into the sky. So beautiful.'

I gazed in awe at the six creatures climbing across the clear full moon, their impressive wings rippling the cloudless sky. To my tired eyes, they looked as though they were on their way to heaven itself. But there was no time for such observations. Moriarty had to be destroyed.

And something was happening to Holmes.

'Watson,' he grunted. 'Help me.'

He had fallen to the ground and was creeping along the path in agony. His fingernails and toenails were bursting through his skin before my eyes. Black hairs shot forth from his hands. Buttons flew from his shirt as his jacket burst open, to reveal a bushy bulldog breast. And his face! It was no longer that of the best and wisest man whom I had ever known. It was the face of an animal, filled with loathing and lust as the sunken eyes glared at me and his slobbering tongue drooled from his snarling, foaming mouth. It was the face of a ravening ... lycanthrope! A loup-garou! A WOLF!'

'Watsey!'

'Awoooooo! Look at me, Watson! Wheeeee! I am at one with the beast. Hee-hee! Ah-hah, ah-hah,' the werewolf howled, stripping off his remaining clothes, grabbing the Luger between his teeth and bounding through the bushes towards the hotel.

'Watsey!'

'... come back, Holmes,' I cried. 'Come ba ... '

'Watsey. Watsey! Wake up! Yer 'aving a daiydream. It's awlmost three bells an' Mr. 'Olmes is dahnstayers in a grahler wayting fer yer tah join 'im fer yer walk.'

'What? What?'

I sat up suddenly and grabbed my newspaper.

'Walk? What walk? Oh, dear me, no. Phew! I shall most certainly not be going out to Richmond today. Be assured of that. My comrades will have to make do without me. Tell Mr. Holmes that he should go on his own. Could you fetch me a double brandy, please, Lily? And switch on the wireless. I would like to hear the state of play in the Test match. Now where *did* I put my pipe?'

6.   Sherlock Holmes And The Hammersmith Hound.

'I need your help again, Holmes. Last clue.'

'Fire away.'

'*Place where feline nests between duck and pussy.* I have an 'o' in the second slot and also as the seventh letter of an eight-letter word.'

'*Location.*'

'Good grief. That is *so* obvious when I see it!' I cried.

'Obvious, and quite elementary, my dear fellow,' he murmured, waving his cherrywood airily in my direction.

I folded the Daily Telegraph and placed it on the basket-chair between us, its cryptic crossword neatly completed. Pausing to relight my dormant cigar, I decided to interrupt the great detective's intense study of Eddington's *The Internal Constitution Of The Stars* once again with a question that had been occupying my mind for some time.

'I say, Holmes. What are we going to do when Lily and Jasper tie the proverbial knot next month?'

'Nothing,' he replied. 'Not a thing. Continue as before. I imagine he will simply move in downstairs with his new wife.'

'So their forthcoming wedding will not affect our domestic arrangements then? Will she continue to be our housekeeper, for instance?'

'I don't see why not. She will have to cook for four, instead of three. Presumably he will take his meals with her.'

'O Lord,' I sighed. 'That will be like having Scotland Yard on our doorstep all the time. Somehow I imagine it will not be long before young Jasper starts to cast his ambitious eyes upon our spacious rooms up here.'

'Perhaps. But he is not his father, is he? It is more likely that he will have the patience to wait until the rooms become available through ... natural wastage. And I am sure that he will be of considerable assistance to us in our future investigations. Always assuming that we have any,' he finished glumly.

'Oh, do cheer up. Of course we will. Listen. That might be one now.'

The front doorbell had chimed frantically several times.

'Quick,' said Holmes, dropping his book and leaping out of the chair. He strode to the window, from which he could gaze, thoughtfully smoking his pipe. 'Grab your paper again and try to look busy. Mutter to yourself in an intelligent manner. Then we shall just about manage to fit our new client into our extremely busy schedule.'

'Bus ... oh, yes. Right. I understand,' I said, picking up the newspaper and rereading the main headlines on Monday, September 6th, 1926: Turkey had allowed civil marriage, the League Of Nations had voted to let Germany enter its hallowed chambers, and Jack Hobbs had scored an undefeated 316 at Lords. Not out! What a batsman!

Soon afterwards we heard the tell-tale *thwack, thwack* of Lily's boots upon the stairs, merging with a much gentler sound, which was more like the tread of a small child.

'Loird Willhiam Trevaor tah see Mr. 'Olmes,' announced Lily grandly.

It was, indeed, a small child. Lord Trevor could hardly have been more than thirteen years of age. Yet his entrance was that of a commanding officer confronting his regiment. The chubby-faced lad was dressed in the customary uniform of a public school-boy, with dark grey blazer – St. Paul's in Hammersmith – white shirt, black tie and light grey flannel shorts.

'Which one of you is Mr. Sherlock Holmes?' he demanded, removing his cap to reveal a crop of fine sandy hair.

'That is my privilege,' answered my old friend, turning around. If Holmes was disappointed that his new client promised nothing more than a possible homework problem – a recurring nightmare of his – he did not show it.

'And I am Dr. Watson,' I said, proffering the sofa to His Lordship. 'Won't you sit down?'

'No, thank you,' he replied solemnly. 'I can only stay for a few minutes. We have our last cricket match of the season within the hour.'

'Oh, really? Who are you playing?' I asked.

'Harrow. It is a decider for the London School's Cup, carried over from last term.'

'And are you a batsman or a bowler?'

'Both, actually. Mr. Holmes, I have come to you with this message because you knew my grandfather some time ago.'

'Ah. I wondered if you were related to Victor,' said Holmes. 'I remember him well. He was one of my few friends at college. His bull-terrier bit me on the ankle one morning on my way to chapel. Victor used to visit me often while I was recovering. He shared my interest in puzzles. In fact, it was *his* father who first set me on the path of detecting. Watson, you may remember how he featured in my first case, the "Gloria Scott" affair.'

'Ahem. Yes. Yes, of course.' In point of fact James Armitage – he changed his name later – had been an escaped criminal who gained his freedom in a mutiny on a prison ship travelling to Australia during the Crimean War. I was sure his great-grandson would be unaware of this, and sincerely hoped that my colleague could maintain some discretion on the subject.

'How did your grandfather die?' continued Holmes.

'Oh, old age, I expect,' replied the boy brightly. Granddad often talked about you when he was alive, though. How you had become the world's greatest detective. He was very proud to have known you.'

Holmes sat down at the table and emptied his pipe onto the remains of his light lunch.

'I am sorry to learn of his passing,' he said. 'Was it in Bengal? I seem to recall that he went to join the Terai tea-planters out there. And he was obviously very successful, if we are now in the company of a member of the aristocracy.'

'No, sir,' replied William, completely unaware of my friend's gentle teasing. 'He had retired from working in the Far East a few years before I was born. Otherwise I might not have known him myself. Actually he only died a few weeks ago. As my father was not interested in attending the reading of the will, our family solicitor Mr. Ramblings did so instead. He had received this beforehand. Apparently it is a bequest to me, but in some form of a code. It states on the outside that it can only be opened by Mister Sherlock Holmes. Hence my presence here. Sir.'

The boy pulled an expensive-looking cream envelope from his breast pocket and handed it across to my colleague. Out of habit, Holmes read the neatly-scripted cover, turned it over, held it up to the light, sniffed it, shook it and examined it minutely with his pocket lens, before opening it. This procedure was borne with some impatience by our juvenile client.

'Perhaps I might leave it with you, and you can let me know your findings at a later date?' he suggested.

'Just a moment, young man,' said Holmes, as he drew out a folded sheet of paper from the envelope with his fingernails. 'Can you confirm the other details of the will? Who inherits the estate at Wennose Park in Norfolk, for instance?'

'It had already been transferred to my father. Then I will get it when he dies. But this has nothing to do with any of that, I believe.' The boy smiled awkwardly, obviously impressed by my friend's knowledge of his family home.

Holmes flicked open the sheet of paper and placed it on the table, using only his fingernails again.

'And do you have any brothers and sisters?'

'No. I am an only child.'

'What about other relatives? Grandmother, aunts, uncles, cousins, mother?'

At the mention of the word mother, the boy's composure wilted a little.

'I have one unmarried aunt, living in India. My ... real mother died a year ago. My father married again shortly afterwards, so I now have a ... step-mother, whose own mother lives with us.'

'Hhmm. All right. You can go. And do try to give up smoking cigarettes before it is too late. Nicotine is such a filthy habit, especially for a budding sportsman. We shall contact you when we have solved your interesting little problem, which presents some very unusual features.'

'And good luck today,' I called after him as he scuttled down the stairs, cap back on head.

'Poor chap,' I remarked, sitting at the table. 'It sounds as though he has noone close to him. The father seems a bit distant and he probably doesn't know his new mother as yet.'

'Nevertheless he is a mature and intelligent young boy. No doubt he will grow up to be as interested in human relationships as your roommate,' commented Holmes drily. 'What do you make of this little beauty?'

He lifted the paper across to me.

'Great heavens! It is another cryptic crossword puzzle!' I exclaimed.

'Not just any old puzzle. It is a rather simplistic version of an *acrostic*, I believe they are called. We have to solve the ... *sixteen* clues and find the first letter of each answer, which will then spell out the final clue. They look like a mixture of language, literature and general knowledge questions. Then the numbers on the back of the paper, when correlated with the letters on the front, may spell out a message of some kind, from Victor himself. That is my reading of it. And we can stop worrying about fingerprints now. I don't think Lord William was that impressed. Although it is an interesting fact that the envelope has been steamed open and resealed afterwards, and the bottom of the paper has been chopped off with a small scissors of the kind normally used by a seamstress. We may be missing a good inch or two. And my name on the envelope has obviously been written by a member of the opposite sex.'

Holmes rubbed his hands together in anticipatory glee.

'In the absence of anything better, Watson, let us to work. I shall need your help on this one, with your intimate knowledge of penmanship and experience of the world around us. Fresh pipes will also be called for. And no. We shall not be involving our housekeeper. At least not *just* yet.'

As usual he had read my mind. I was about to suggest that Lily Hudson help us out. Despite her position within our household, she had shown an impressive instinct for solving ciphers in some recent cases. But at least this crossword puzzle might occupy my friend for a while, and take his mind off his cocaine habit, which was becoming a problem again.

I filled my pipe with ship's tobacco and lit it. Then I sat gazing blankly at the acrostic puzzle. First the clues:

1. *London picnic area reduced, holding feed. (5)*
2. *Quantity of amalgam in Italy altered by the end of chat. (10)*
3. *Film the french body part for overhead plant. (9)*
4. *Radiant flier has a little cantaloupe in its belly. (5)*
5. *Not giving name back to an incompletely finished rodent. (9)*
6. *Stocky kentish ewes yammer regularly, mixing with Ram's horn. (6,5)*
7. *Donor goes without one to become pliable. (8)*
8. *A numeric fixing of male digits. (8)*
9. *A natural process – area of study seen at end of tavern. (12)*
10. *Popular story from novelist who begins with a bayonet, river inside, severe-sounding. (8,6)*
11. *Air that lives on a stove. (4,2,3,5)*
12. *Unbreakable centuries, a novel set in the North. (4,5)*
13. *Notice of a conclusion. (8)*
14. *Togetherness and freedom, a poem by sleuth namesake. (5,3,7)*
15. *Clean kitchen finally, having had breakfast. (6)*

16. *Licentious series of books showing up after a number of years. (8)*

Normally it took me some time before I could change gear mentally to solve certain crosswords, and this time was no exception, despite having finished the Telegraph Cryptic. Whereas Holmes just leapt right in with both sides of that terrific brain fizzing.

'Got the first one, Watson. Five letters. *London picnic area reduced, holding feed.* It is surely **heath**. *H* at the beginning and the end for Hampstead Heath *reduced*, with *eat* inside, meaning feed. Your turn.'

'Just a minute. Let me see. Now. Eh, *Notice of a conclusion* is probably **obituary**, don't you think? And *Film the French body part for overhead plant* must be **mistletoe**. Both rather obvious.'

'Indeed. I shall put them in,' said Holmes. 'Next. *Quantity of amalgam in Italy altered by the end of chat.* Could be a chemistry clue. Chat could be *talk*, without the *t* at the beginning. Lots of scientific words begin with *alk,* and if we shuffle the letters from *in Italy* around, we get ... **alkalinity**! Meaning 'the quantitative capacity of an aqueous solution to neutralize an acid.'

'Whatever you say. Number seven is a regular Telegraph clue,' I responded. '*Donor goes without one to become pliable.* The answer is **supplier**, also a *donor*. Without an *i*, or a *1,* it becomes suppler, or more *pliable*.'

'*A numeric fixing of male digits* has to be **manicure**. Self-explanatory, I believe.'

'And an anagram of *a numeric*,' I added. 'Then *Unbreakable centuries, a novel set in the North.* This is Charles Dickens, of course. **Hard Times** is set outside London, in the North of England, unusually for him.'

'*Togetherness and freedom, a poem by sleuth namesake:*

    "Flag of the heroes who left us their glory,
    Borne through their battle-fields' thunder and flame,
    Blazoned in song and illumined in story,
    Wave o'er us all who inherit their fame!" '

'Is that Yeats?' I queried uneasily. Holmes had developed a jarring interest in literature and poetry during his many lonely nights on the Sussex Downs. For some reason, he seemed eerily attached to the Irish poet.

'I know of no detectives called Yeats, Watson. But I am familiar with the work called **Union And Liberty**, by one Oliver Wendell Holmes!'

'Never heard of him. *Clean kitchen finally, having had breakfast.* This is **neaten**. The last letter of kitche*n*, followed by *eaten*, meaning *clean*.'

'Half-way there,' said Holmes. '*Air that lives on a stove. Air* usually means song. Four, two, three, five. Something *on the* something?'

'Another word for *stove* is range,' I suggested. '**Home on the range?**'

'Watson, you excel. What about *Licentious series of books showing up after a number of years?*'

'Cryptic crosswords often start with a synonym. So the answer could mean *licentious*. Series of books could be the New Testament – nt – and the number of years might be – decade?'

'**Decadent**!' Holmes noted down the word excitedly. 'Upon my word. We have only five clues left, Watson.'

'Number ten – *Popular story from novelist who begins with a bayonet, river inside, severe-sounding* – is **Tristram Shandy**.'

'Why? Please explain,' demanded Holmes.

'Well, Laurence Sterne wrote it. Stern means *severe*. Then his Christian name is made up of a word meaning bayonet – *lance* – with the name of a river – *ure* – inside.'

'*Radiant flier has a little cantaloupe in its belly.* Probably the name of a bird. *Radiant* could mean brightly coloured. And another word for *belly* is *maw*. Got it! **Macaw!**'

'Well done, Holmes! Only numbers 5,6,9 left. Let me see. *Stocky kentish ewes yammer regularly, mixing with Ram's horn.* Regularly usually means every second letter, which would be *y, m, e* from *yammer*. Add them to *ram's horn* for an anagram of a place in Kent.'

'**Romney Marsh**! The Wetlands where sheep are kept,' finished Holmes. 'Good show, old fellow. Down to two. *A natural process – area of study seen at end of tavern.* End of tavern is the letter *n*. *Area of study* could be ... *science*? Add that to *seen* and *n* for an anagram of *a natural process*. Hah! It is about us, Watson! We who are growing old. **Insenescence**. Nearly there.'

'And I believe I have the answer to clue number 5, the last one,' I stated. '*Not giving name back to an incompletely finished rodent.* It ends in *mous*, with *nope* reversed and a *y* before it – **eponymous**, meaning to name something.'

'Excellent! Let me see what we have at the end,' exclaimed Holmes.

Once the great detective had entered all of the solutions, the crossword looked like this:

H	E	A	T	H										
1	2	3	4	5										
A	L	K	A	L	I	N	I	T	Y					
6	7	8	9	10	11	12	13	14	15					

M 16	I 17	S 18	T 19	L 20	E 21	T 22	O 23	E 24					
M 25	A 26	C 27	A 28	W 29									
E 30	P 31	O 32	N 33	Y 34	M 35	O 36	U 37	S 38					
R 39	O 40	M 41	N 42	E 43	Y 44	M 45	A 46	R 47	S 48	H 49			
S 50	U 51	P 52	P 53	L 54	I 55	E 56	R 57						
M 58	A 59	N 60	I 61	C 62	U 63	R 64	E 65						
I 66	N 67	S 68	E 69	N 70	E 71	S 72	C 73	E 74	N 75	C 76	E 77		
T 78	R 79	I 80	S 81	T 82	R 83	A 84	M 85	S 86	H 87	A 88	N 89	D 90	Y 91
H 92	O 93	M 94	E 95	O 96	N 97	T 98	H 99	E 100	R 101	A 102	N 103	G 104	E 105
H 106	A 107	R 108	D 109	T 110	I 111	M 112	E 113	S 114					
O 115	B 116	I 117	T 118	U 119	A 120	R 121	Y 122						
U 123	N 124	I 125	O 126	N 127	A 128	N 129	D 130	L 131	I 132	B 133	E 134	R 135	T 136	Y 137
N 138	E 139	A 140	T 141	E 142	N 143								
D 144	E 145	C 146	A 147	D 148	E 149	N 150	T 151						

'There you go, old chap. We have put the beast to bed in record time,' claimed Holmes, puffing out a cloud of dense shag in satisfaction. 'Our final clue is down the left-hand side. It reads HAMMERSMITH HOUND. But what that means as a bequest, is the guess of anybody.'

161

'Maybe a dog to keep the poor little fellow company?' I suggested hopefully.

'Not if I know my old pal Victor, it ain't. He would not go to the trouble of creating this monster unless there was some *point* to it,' muttered the great detective. 'There is rather more to this than you might imagine, Watson. Let us now align the numbers on the back of the paper with the letters in the crossword. The coded message will then set us on our way to a complete solution.'

I sat back as Holmes worked his way through the correlation, feeling sure that only one person could do the job of making sense of the following sequence of numbers: 1, 23, 7, 16, 2, 18, 137, 126, 123, 94, 63, 50, 78, 144, 145, 48, 82, 57, 32, 91, 136, 87, 139, 127, 142, 38, 141, 140, 12, 130, 64, 65, 68, 62, 119, 56, 40, 37, 83, 27, 32, 51, 42, 98, 39, 44.

When he had finished, he read out the message to me: '*Holmes, you must destroy the nest and rescue our country.*'

'So, Watson. What do you make of that?' he asked.

'I have not the slightest idea,' I replied. 'Your old friend seemed to think that the United Kingdom was in danger from a nest of some kind. But where is it? And what does it contain? And why all this convoluted, secret trickery to warn you? He could just as easily have sent you a more detailed telegram with the uncoded message on it, before he passed away. Or telephoned? Or even dropped around to visit us, if he could?'

'Exactly. It must be something to do with his family. Perhaps he is trying to protect someone. Kindly pull down my index under the letter H and see if there is anything of interest recorded under Hammersmith or Hound, or both? Not the Baskerville one, obviously.'

But my friend's carefully annotated notes on all H subjects of past merit held no insight whatsoever. With that he drew his chair across the room towards the window and turned to me.

'I shall need some time alone to think about this, old fellow, if you don't mind,' he suggested gravely. 'There may be dark and murky waters here. I shall work better in silence.'

'Oh, of course. Let us hope that it is not just some kind of joke from a dying man. Perhaps the future of our country really *is* at stake. Eh, Holmes, should we not inform the good Lestrade of this warning? After all, Scotland Yard may already know something about this *Hammersmith Hound.*'

'No. Not until we have some more definite data on the subject. The Yard functions by bureaucratic procedures alone. There is no room for individual genius there, as you well know. They would simply laugh at the idea of a crossword being the source of data about a crime.'

I was quite happy to gain some respite from puzzling letters and numbers for a while and return to reading the dailies. When they had been exhausted, I continued to work on my speech for Lily and Jasper's wedding. As I was giving our housekeeper away, I needed to come up with some ready witticisms on the nature of marriage. What about old Abe Lincoln's '*Marriage is neither heaven nor hell, it is simply purgatory?*' Maybe not. '*Happy unions exist when the man is strong enough to permit the woman the illusion that she is in control of the relationship*'. Definitely not. Our housekeeper will surely be the mistress of that union!

My colleague spent the remainder of the afternoon infusing the sitting room with a London peculiar of blue murky smog while he applied his brain to Victor Trevor's message. I could not get a sensible word from him. By 5pm I was forced to leave the house to stretch my legs around an autumnal Regent's Park and to clear my lungs with some badly needed fresh air.

When I arrived back at 221B Baker Street later that evening, Holmes was nowhere to be found. Lily explained that a person resembling the great detective, dressed as a chef, complete with reversible double breasted white jacket, check patterned trousers and high starched white toque, had left the building in a tremendous hurry some time beforehand. Knowing his propensity for disguises, and wondering where he unearthed his outfits, I had no alternative other than to wait for some word from him about the late Victor Trevor's warning – '... *destroy the nest and rescue our country.*'

I was polishing off the remains of my haddock kedgeree the following morning when I received the first hint of his activities. My friend must have been up for most of the night, as he emerged from his bedroom bleary-eyed, with angry red splotches speckling his face, and dressed in his customary mousy dressing-gown. He glanced at the laden breakfast table and groaned.

'Oh, dear God. If I never see food again, it will be too soon,' he muttered, stumbling over to the mantlepiece. He gathered his dottles, rubbed them together in the palms of his hands, fed the shredded tobacco into his blackened clay pipe and lit it, before slumping onto the sofa.

'I hear that you have become a master of the culinary arts,' I said, pushing my plate away.

He ignored my facetious comment.

'Have you ever heard of *Yersinia Pestis*?'

'No,' I replied.

'Well, as a doctor, you certainly should have. It has caused at least three human plague pandemics. The first was known as the Plague Of Justinian in the 6th century, named after the Byzantine Emperor. Then there was the Black Death, which wiped out a third of the population of Europe between the 14th and 17th centuries. The last epidemic in the 19th century killed more than twelve million people in India and China alone.'

'But what exactly is it?' I asked, trying to ignore the queasiness rising inside my stomach, and the growing ache in my old leg wound.

Holmes yawned loudly. 'To be blunt, a deadly virus carried from rats to fleas to humans, originating mainly in the orient, probably China.'

Wide-eyed, I sat down opposite him in the basket-chair.

'Chinese rat fleas? Is that what Victor Trevor is warning us about? This *pestis*?'

Holmes shifted uncomfortably. Then he swung his legs around onto the sofa, ran his fingers through his thick grey hair, leaned back, drew deeply on his pipe and sighed.

'I do not know, Watson. Yesterday, after much intense concentration on the crossword problem, I decided that I did not have enough data to work with. One cannot make an omelette without eggs. There seemed little point in trying to guess the meaning of the *Hammersmith Hound* clue, although it is probably safe to assume that it has some criminal context. I needed to know more about Victor's life. How he spent his time abroad, where he worked, why he returned, the real cause of his death.

More about his family life. His son, the boy's father, for instance. What is his occupation? The puzzle was just a warning, nothing else. Yet Victor would have expected me to do something about it, to benefit his grandson in some way. Perhaps even to save the boy's life, as well as everybody else's. You seemed to have vanished, so I was forced to proceed alo..'

'I needed some fresh air,' I protested.

'...ne. I wanted you to pursue the family angle. Maybe pay a visit to the Norfolk estate under some guise, a survey of old country houses for an agent's magazine, or suchlike, and talk to the boy's father, whom I strongly suspect of having steamed open the envelope. Meanwhile I would work on the clue. Where better to start than in Hammersmith itself? And what is the fount of all gossip about crimes?'

'Eh, a pub?'

'Precisely. I remembered having done a good turn once for the owner of The Old Ship, down by the Thames. Launcelot Oddways was only too happy to allow me to pretend to be a cook in his establishment for one night, as gratitude for having found a treasured sports trophy his wife had tried to hock. It was grounds for a subsequent divorce hearing. He has remarried since then, and is perfectly content with his new Asian wife.'

'But where did you get your chef disguise?' I asked.

'Hah! Obviously you and your readers do not know everything about me, my Boswell. It was no disguise, merely an outfit I used to wear when I was an undergraduate, and working part-time as a commis-chef in a local restaurant near the British Museum to finance my studies. I had quite forgotten the sheer exhaustion that arises from such work.'

He ran his fingers delicately over his face.

'And how devilishly hot a kitchen can become.'

'And did you find anything out about the clue, the *Hammersmith Hound*?' I asked patiently.

'Oh, yes indeed. There was not much to be discovered in the kitchen itself, although I did try. All the other chefs were from Holland and spoke very little English. On my break I started chatting to a group of grizzled old seadogs who looked as though they only set foot on land occasionally to pick up their post. One of them actually had a wooden pegleg and another an eye-patch. But when I mentioned the words *Hammersmith Hound*, they clammed up immediately. I might as well have accused them of running guns to Spain. It took all my guile and quite a few florins, as well as several rounds of the devil's brew to prise the information I needed from them.'

Holmes paused, as he sent a spiral of grey smoke drifting towards the ceiling.

'The *Hammersmith Hound* was the name of a motorised sailing vessel that came aground off the Norfolk coast, near the village of Brancaster, about fifteen years ago. Rumour among the fishing fraternity had it that the boat was cursed. Four Indian gentlemen were found dead on board when it floated in on the tide. They had black pustules on their faces, huge lumps on their necks and under their arms and many other signs of a horrible disease. Being a close-knit community and deeply superstitious folk, the villagers buried the quartet swiftly and kept quiet about the deaths, in case any publicity might adversely affect their livelihoods. My feeling is that the dead men may have been victims of a plague, such as that caused by *Yersinia Pestis*. When I returned to Baker Street, I passed much of the night researching the subject in my *Pathology Of Parasitic Fevers*. Usually the fleas kill the rats they feed off and then turn to humans for their nourishment, thus infecting other fleas who will travel from person to person, etc., etc., But it can also be airborne, of course.'

'And do you really believe this nest of Victor's was aboard that boat, Holmes?' I asked.

'Was, and maybe still *is*. We must discover the truth. What are our facts? *One*: The name of the boat. *Two*: Its location off the coast of Norfolk, which my fishermen friends gave me. One of them even drew me a rough map. *Three*: The family home, also in Norfolk. *Four*: Victor's return home from the *Far East*. According to the boy, that was around the same time as the boat's arrival. He might have relocated from India to China. Hence a possible connection to rat fleas. And rats can prosper in mud, of course,' he added as an afterthought.

Holmes summoned his incredible reserves of strength to propel his body up from the sofa and head towards his bedroom, flinging his dressing-gown to the floor as he went.

'Check the times of the trains from Liverpool Street to Norfolk, Watson, will you? We will then continue on to Brancaster for a thorough search of the boat. I shall arrange for Wiggins and a few of his pals to meet us at Brancaster Staithe station, with the necessary dredging equipment and some petrol-soaked rags. Without giving them any of the gory details, of course. Put on your wellingtons and bring along that bull pup of yours, old chap. Fully loaded, of course. I shall be carrying my stick-sword and my trusty persuader. All good for killing rats, I should imagine.'

'Dredging? Petrol-soaked rags? Killing rats? Holmes, have you lost your mind? What about the deadly virus?' I called after him, panic-stricken. 'This *Yersinia Pestis*? Surely we must inform the proper authorities? What if we accidently cause another Black Death to hit Great Britain? This is utterly irresponsible! Oh, and while we're on the subject. What if some Chinese rat fleas jump onto us and *we* catch the damn plague and die horrible deaths ourselves?

Holmes reappeared at the door of his bedroom, attaching a collar to his shirt. He glared at me fiercely.

'Would you prefer that your young cricketer friend catches it first? No? I did not think so. Remember the bequest, Watson,' he stated firmly. '*You must destroy the nest and rescue our country.*'

'There it is!' cried Holmes.

He was checking his map and pointing ahead with his stick-sword at the battered remains of the upper portion of a sailing craft that was sticking out of the sludge at an obtuse angle. Faded black paint peeled from its side and flickered in the day's stiff breeze. I could just make out the last three letters of a word – *und*. The tip of a split discoloured masthead rig lay buried near its hull. This shell of a boat was not alone in its decrepitude, being surrounded by a number of neighbourly wrecks in their muddy graveyard. Beyond the boat cemetery stretched the forbidding grey marshlands of North Norfolk, riddled with swishing willows, thin rivulets of water and reedswamp vegetation, behind which water hens croaked nervously at each other.

Throughout our trip, Holmes had completely ignored my misgivings about our foolhardy plan to explore the

Hammersmith Hound. I particularly did not think it fair to keep Wiggins and his crew ignorant of the dangers involved. But in the face of his continued silence I had to cease my complaints and hope that if any of us became infected, some smart chemist with a vested interest might invent a vaccine or antibiotic to save us.

'Wiggins!' shouted my colleague. 'Come on, man! Go to work! Pull her up!'

I stood well back and leaned against a nearby skiff to rest my throbbing leg – even my old shoulder wound from the Battle Of Maiwand, which was supposed to be fully healed, had begun to twinge – as the four workmen attached metal grappling hooks to cleats at the front and side of the Hammersmith Hound. Then they placed a winch behind the vessel and Wiggins started to wind. The hooks tautened and strained, but nothing happened. There was no movement from the boat. Wiggins wiped the sweat from his forehead with a filthy rag. He tried again. Still no luck. A third effort produced the same result. Then one of the other workmen, a giant of a labourer, stepped up behind him and indicated that he would take over.

'It's all yours, Tarzan,' grumbled Wiggins. 'Work away.'

The colossus grabbed the handle of the winch with his massive paw. Holding his other hand beneath it for leverage, he grimaced as he strove to pull upwards. After a short interval, the winch began to creak. I held my breath as the front of the boat rose slowly from its mired captivity with a nauseating sucking noise that reminded me of those awful trenches in the Great War and having to dig corpses out of the mud.

It took a while, but once the hulk of the *Hammersmith Hound* had been hauled out and had risen to a sufficient height, its own weight caused it to cant over onto its side, and squish on top of the marsh. I was relieved to see that no rats came leaping immediately out of the subsequent gash in the wreck.

Holmes squelched over to it and signalled for me to join him by the boat. I did so reluctantly, holding a handkerchief firmly to my mouth and praying inwardly for salvation. I also kept a sharp eye out for any sudden movements on the deck.

My colleague climbed onto the hull and kicked open the door into the cabin. As there was still no sound of squealing, I followed him cautiously down.

'Stay where you are, Watson,' instructed Holmes, something I was only too happy to do. He fired up a vesta match, removed his persuader from his pocket, and progressed out of my view and into the bowels of the boat. At that moment, an indescribably evil odour assaulted my nostrils, as though I was being attacked by a family of skunks. It forced me back up to the side of the deck and out onto the marsh. Wiggins and company noticed it also, and retreated swiftly to the Brancaster road.

I did not understand how my friend could tolerate the foul stench from that filthy hole, until I realised that he would need to establish its source, and his supremely rational mind would have developed a suitably clever method of coping with such discomforts.

It was several minutes before he emerged from the cabin hurriedly, carrying a cardboard box underneath one arm and his nostrils pinched between two fingers from the other hand. He glanced around in puzzlement before spying the four workers on the path.

'Right, Wiggins,' he called over nasally. 'You can place the rag inside now and set fire to the boat.'

The sole remaining active member of the Baker Street Irregulars – the others were all in jail – decided to copy Holmes, and moved cautiously towards the boat holding his nose. While he finished his job, Holmes set the box down on top of a nearby skiff.

'Do not worry, Watson,' he smiled. 'This does not contain a family of rodents. And if there were any Chinese rat fleas inside the *Hammersmith Hound*, they appear to have long since flown the coop. Those rodents in the cabin had been dead for many years. They may have died at the same time as the sailors. The boat was not a haven for *Yersinia Pestis*, or for any other virus, to my knowledge. But it did contain a virulent nest of overblown flowery prose.'

Like a magician, Holmes lifted the lid off the box, to reveal a pile of yellowing magazines. He flicked through them with his hand, sending up a fine sprinkling of dust and revealing the word Strand in their titles, like an early motion picture projector. His eyes twinkled as he joked, 'Perhaps the rats died of boredom, Watson.'

I ignored his jibe and took a closer look at the magazines. I was simultaneously relieved and puzzled.

'You do realise, Holmes, that they are all copies of the *same* edition of the magazine, the one that contains an early adventure of yours, published in July, 1891. It was called 'A Scandal In Bohemia'. And just look at this.'

I held out the page where the story started with the following words: 'To Sherlock Holmes she is always *the* woman.' The sentence was underlined in faded red ink. A quick check of the other copies showed a similar high-lighting in each one.

Holmes blanched visibly at this revelation. The woman in question was, of course, the adventuress Irene Adler, the only female to have outwitted the great detective, and consequently, the only one that he held in any sort of regard. It had not been romantic love that he felt for her, more respect for an intellectual equal. She had married a lawyer named Godfrey Norton and left the country all those years ago. To my knowledge, neither of us had heard anything of her since. But I was aware that Holmes still kept her framed photograph on his bedside locker and so I could not resist a small degree of revenge for his taunt.

'You do remember her, don't you, Holmes?'

'Yes, of course, Watson.' He smiled grimly. 'But we are not finished with this case yet. The nest on the boat may be burning, but we still need some explanation for Trevor's puzzle. Maybe *rescue our country* is a separate request, and has nothing whatsoever to do with the rats.'

'I really don't see what else we can do for the young Lord,' I complained, eager to get back to Baker Street in time for dinner.

Holmes handed the box of magazines over to me and gazed across at the burning boat.

'It is time we paid that visit to the Trevor family estate. I am convinced that the answer to this puzzle lies within its walls. You can get on back to Baker Street if you want to, old chap, and spend the evening rereading your highfalutin' story about the King Of Bohemia and his mistaken liaison with Miss Adler.'

'Oh, no. As usual, *whither thou goest, I will go,*' I replied, somewhat nettled. 'Let Wiggins take this box back with him.'

'Good old Watson. Ever true. We should be able to get a Beardmore taxi-cab out to the house. I know you hate the things, but it is too far for a growler. You never know. The Trevors might be about to dine and may be only too happy to invite the two famous detectives to join them at table. And bring one of those tawdry rags with you.'

Holmes was correct when he assumed that his old pal had been successful in his career abroad. Wennose Park was a truly grand estate off the road to Norwich. It had a woodland setting, complete with a large lake spotted with swans, a stilted boathouse, statues, fountains, urns, a water tower, several follies, a walled garden, terraced lawns and a greenhouse that ran the full length of the Edwardian country house. The wind had died down and the sun was vanishing behind the sizeable oak trees as we observed these noble features on the last leg of our thirty-mile journey, up the driveway to the cobblestoned entrance and a welcoming chorus of frenetic baying hounds. They had to be controlled and ordered back to their kennels in a nearby yard by a fuming red-faced lad, dressed smartly in tartan shirt, green corduroy trousers, leather riding boots, and with a shotgun slung over his shoulder. Only then could we escape from the Beardmore beast. After a small fuss about the ridiculous cost of the journey, we had finally paid off our cabbie when the same angry young man returned from the stables.

'Well? What do you want?' he demanded, pointing his shotgun directly at my friend.

'My name is Sherlock Holmes, and this is my companion, Dr. Watson.'

If he expected this introduction to have a calming effect upon the wild-eyed child, Holmes was disappointed.

'Never heard of either of you. This is a private residence. I will give you exactly five seconds to answer my question, before I blast you pair of old buggers to kingdom co ...'

Holmes moved like lightning to wrest the firearm from the aggressive kennelboy's arm, swivel it around, and point it back at him.

'I shall ask the questions from now on, thank you,' he said. 'We would like to visit the owner of this estate to discuss a matter of some importance with him. So just run along and find him for us, will you? Like the faithful young bugger you are. There's a good boy. Go on. Move! That is, if you don't want some of your blood to spoil that colourful outfit.'

The frightened youth ran over to the main entrance and disappeared into the entrails of the huge mansion. Holmes handed me the shotgun as he followed him.

'Hold onto this, Watson. We may need it later. And be ready for anything.'

We had reached the steps leading up to the portico at the hall entrance when a tall young woman appeared at the door. She boasted curly auburn locks, wore an elegant pink evening dress and was smoking a purple Turkish cigarette in a jade holder. There was something oddly familiar about her pale oval features, but for the life of me I could not place my finger upon it. She glanced in amusement at me and my shotgun, which I promptly broke, taking out the two cartridges and pocketing them, before pointing the weapon at the ground for the sake of her safety. Then she turned to Holmes.

'I take it you are the one and only Sherlock Holmes,' she said. 'The great detective. You are a little older than I imagined.'

Ignoring this sleight, Holmes enquired, 'And whom do I have the pleasure of addressing?'

'I am Lady Violet Trevor, wife to Lord Sebastian Trevor.'

'Oh, excellent. The step-mother herself. Then perhaps you might care to explain this.'

Holmes produced the crossword paper from a pocket and waved it in front of her face. She flinched with annoyance, but made an attempt to read the clues before handing it back to him in puzzlement and murmuring, 'You had better come inside and explain yourselves. It is all right, Richard.'

The young man scowled when I handed him his gun. He stood to one side as we followed Her Ladyship through the colonnaded hall and into a vast conservatory that looked as though it had been borrowed from Kew Gardens. Blooming hydrangeas of various hues lined the walls. There was an octagonal table in the corner at one end, with the remains of an evening meal upon it, waiting to be cleared. I had a faint hope that some form of nourishment might be on the horizon, but it was not to be. Instead, our hostess bid us take our seats at the table and introduced us to the other sole occupant, a tired-looking middle-aged woman, who wore a pince-nez and was knitting what looked to me like an extremely long red scarf.

'Mother,' said Lady Violet. 'We have visitors. This is Dr. Watson, and I believe that you have already met the consulting detective, Sherlock Holmes.'

In all my time with Holmes, and over many criminal enquiries that had oscillated between the extremes of violent murder and petty larceny, I had never seen him at a loss for words. This was the first such occasion.

'Hello, Sherlock,' said Irene Adler, resting her knitting upon her lap. 'It has been many long years, has it not?'

Holmes made a choking sound, like a suppressed growl in a dog's throat. Then he struggled to regain his composure by patting his pockets in a desperate search for his pipe, and giggling slightly. I decided to help him out by joining him.

'Do you ladies mind if we smoke?' I enquired.

'Not at all,' replied Lady Violet.

Once we had filled our pipes and were puffing away, Holmes made a valiant effort to recover from his initial shock and regain control of the situation.

'To be precise, Mrs ... Norton, it is thirty-five years since our last encounter, in the matter of the photograph of you with the late King Of Bohemia. A possible blackmail, if I remember correctly?'

'My favourite story of them all!' exclaimed Lady Violet.

'And one that was so admirably captured by Dr. Watson in the Strand Magazine,' added Irene Adler. 'Alas, Sherlock, I am no longer Mrs Norton. I resumed my maiden name after the death of my husband several years ago.'

'I am sorry to hear that,' murmured Holmes and I in unison.

'But Mother, this is not a social visit,' said Lady Violet. 'Mr. Holmes has come in connection with some sort of crossword puzzle. Can you show it to my mother, please?'

Holmes leaned forward and handed the slip of paper to Irene Adler.

'Lord William Trevor came to our rooms at Baker Street yesterday and asked us to investigate this bequest to him from his grandfather, who was an old friend of mine many years ago,' explained Holmes. 'We have solved the acrostic puzzle itself easily enough. Here is the solution.'

Holmes handed over another sheet of paper, before continuing.

'But we do not yet know why Victor Trevor would leave behind such a strange heritage for his grandson. Nor how we can fulfil its demand that we *destroy the nest and rescue our country.*'

While the two ladies examined the crossword and its solution closely, Holmes outlined our efforts to date, with the discovery of the *Hammersmith Hound*, its contents and its destruction. At his suggestion, I then handed over my copy of the relevant Strand Magazine to Lady Violet.

'Oh, but this is one of my collection!' she squealed.

'Do explain, please,' asked Holmes.

'When I was growing up in Calcutta, I used to buy copies of the magazine, in order to read those wonderful stories of yours, Dr. Watson. Because my mother had featured in one of them, I acquired many copies of it and stored them in a box beneath my bed. I even underlined the first sentence in each one! Oh, Mr. Holmes, was my mother really *the* woman?'

Holmes actually blushed. It was a thing to see.

'I fear that my colleague is prone to the occasional exaggeration in the cause of verisimilitude,' he stated firmly, unable to meet Irene Adler's amused gaze. 'To return to the bequest, Lady Violet. When did you come back from India? How did you become involved with Victor Trevor's son? And is that particular gentleman at home? Perhaps he can shed some light on this singular affair.'

'My husband normally stays in his flat in London during the week,' replied Lady Violet. 'He is a Director of Kettlewell Bullen, who manage the affairs of the Joonktolleetea Tea Company in Upper Assam. His life revolves around his work, and he leaves the running of the country estate to me and my mother. Only in an absolute emergency would he change his routine.'

Lady Violet paused to insert another foul-smelling Turkish cigarette into her holder.

'Despite the ten-year difference in our ages, I suppose you could say that Sebastian and I grew up together,' she continued. 'We Nortons lived next door to the Trevors in Calcutta, which was the second city of the British Empire then. My father worked as a lawyer to the tea company partly-owned by your friend Victor. I had noone of my own age to play with, as I was being schooled at home by a governess. He was in his teens when I was a precocious seven-year-old tomboy, interested in almost everything. Sports were his big hobby. He taught me how to fish in the nearby River Hooghly, how to play hockey and tennis in the local British Clubs, how to sail a boat, how to climb trees, and ... oh, *lots* of other activities. I suppose I had a schoolgirl crush on him as well. Anyway, cutting this long story short, when the political situation in Calcutta got tricky they returned to England. We

179

followed them about fifteen years ago and I was devastated to discover that he had married a local girl from Norfolk, and was living in this grand house.'

She paused again, and continued in an innocent tone of voice that suggested she still could not quite comprehend what had happened to her.

'But all good things come to those who wait, I suppose. Although it is sad that his wife had to die before we could be together.'

'How did his first wife die?' enquired Holmes.

'A car crash,' answered Irene Adler, smiling wearily.

'Hhmm. And how did you travel back from India, Lady Violet?' asked Holmes brusquely.

'On a P&O liner. That was the norm then.'

'Can you remember what happened to your box of magazines?' continued Holmes.

'No! I had forgotten all about them until just now! They were supposed to be packed as part of our luggage. Mother?'

Irene Adler removed her pince-nez and placed both pieces of paper down on the table. She looked extremely ill to me – cancer was my quess – and with not that long to go. She had to clear her throat noisily before speaking.

'There was no room for the box in our luggage, my dear,' she replied. 'However. We had four very faithful servants in that house, all of whom were most upset to see us go, and whose lives may have been in danger afterwards if they had stayed. They wanted to come with us, but we could not afford to pay their way. So I gave them our old sailing boat, together with some supplies, and renamed it after our destination in London. They were supposed to follow us back to England, taking your box with them.'

'All the way from India?' I interjected in disbelief.

'It has been done, believe it or not. And the engine was still functioning perfectly well. Nevertheless, I did try to argue them out of their foolish plan. They would not listen to me. Obviously the boat made it eventually, although they appear to have caught some horrible disease along the way. But the vessel was not called the *Hammersmith Hound*. It was the *Hammersmith Bound*.'

Holmes did not react immediately. He sat frozen in his chair, pipe in mid-air, half-way to his mouth. Then he put it down hurriedly and grabbed the papers and studied them closely together.

'Does this mean that we have got one of the clues wrong, Holmes?' I ventured. *Hard Times*?

'No,' interrupted Irene Adler. 'But someone has cut off the bottom of the paper, leading to a missing clue, as well as the final word of the message itself. It should read *Hammersmith Hounds* down the left-hand side, and the message should be: *Holmes, destroy the nest and rescue our country estate.* I should know, because I created it. And I sent it to you.'

Holmes stared at her in astonishment.

'Oh, my good Lord,' I groaned.

'Mother!' cried Lady Violet.

'Do you hunt, Sherlock?' enquired Irene Adler, with an exhausted sigh.

'No,' replied Holmes. 'I do not ride with the ... the hounds. But why? Why did you send this message to me via young William, pretending that it came from Victor, might I ask?'

'I am dying, Sherlock,' she replied, ignoring her daughter's sniffles. 'My doctor has informed me that it is now a matter of weeks, rather than months. A tumour within the brain. Inoperable. Before I depart this world, I wish to secure Violet's future and that of the estate she has married into. Although we are obviously not in straitened circumstances, there is a danger that we might lose Wennose Park. He would never admit it, but Lord Sebastian does not earn enough money to maintain a property of this size. I have had to contribute most of my inheritance to the account. As well as running a small meat farm, we survive largely by the revenue we make from the monthly running of the private foxhound pack. We named them the Hammersmith Hounds, after the place we lived in so happily when we first returned to England. Violet, please hand me that glass of water.'

Irene Adler had begun to gasp as she grabbed a small box of green pills from her handbag, and swallowed one with the water. Once she had recovered her breath, she continued.

'I am sure you are aware that, in the noble art of venery, the hounds hunt by the scent of the fox. Well, our last few meets have been rendered virtually impossible by the damage done by a nest of Eurasian eagle-owls, based in our barn. The four birds hibernate during the day, but attack the cubs at night, and leave their remains spread around the demesne. The hounds then lead the meet astray on the basis of a false scent, and the hunt is forced to end prematurely. Unless we solve this problem, we have been informed that the East Anglian Bloodhounds Association will take their business elsewhere. We have tried many ways of getting rid of these creatures, short of burning down the barn, but they have all failed to date. As a last resort, I imagined that my artful old nemesis could be our possible saviour.'

'But why can not your ... son-in-law deal with this simple problem? Or that obnoxious young brat of a dog handler? Why me?' demanded Holmes.

'Yes, Mother,' said Lady Violet. 'Why send for Mr. Holmes in this complicated manner?'

Irene Adler replaced her pince-nez on her nose coyly.

'I felt that you would not come if I simply asked you, because of our past ... association. As well as solving this problem for us, I had hoped that the puzzle would bring you here, so that I could meet with you one last time, before ... the end, so to speak,' she replied. 'You know, just for old times' sake. And to say goodbye.'

'To say goodbye,' repeated Holmes, almost to himself.

'The eagle-owl is indeed a most dangerous raptor,' I volunteered, in order to break a somewhat eerie silence. I feared that the great detective might not be able to cope with the emotions aroused by a dying Irene Adler.

'What?' muttered Holmes. 'Oh, yes, Watson. The owls and the foxes, and the Hammersmith Hounds. Nothing to do with Chinese rat fleas after all, eh?'

My distressed friend stood up abruptly and addressed Irene Adler.

'Of course I will do my utmost to help you. Perhaps your daughter would be kind enough to show me the exact location of this nest, while my hungry colleague remains with you and partakes of some tea and cakes, courtesy of your maid.'

I protested at this rude suggestion that my appetite might be of more importance than the problem at hand, but acquiesced eventually to the comforting ministrations of Irene Adler and her well-endowed maid, Veronica, who produced a toothsome array of buttered scones and jam for my enjoyment, with a pot of scalding Earl Grey.

Holmes returned to the conservatory with Lady Violet as I was finishing my third cup of tea. During his absence, Irene Adler had entertained me with her detailed knowledge of the Holmes canon, which she had enjoyed reading all her life. She was even able to point out a couple of plotting inconsistencies which had escaped my usually sharp editing eye.

'Mr. Holmes has a suggestion to make about the owls, mother,' said Lady Violet, as she lit yet another of her abominable Turkish cigarettes.

'You need a bal-chatri trap,' said my colleague, who remained standing in front of Irene Adler, tapping his fingers on the table for emphasis. It was apparent to me that his impatient demeanour indicated a growing boredom with the puzzle of the Hammersmith Hound. Combined, perhaps, with a degree of confusion as to how to deal with his conflicting emotions regarding *the* woman, and her pending demise.

'And what exactly is that?' Irene asked.

'It is designed specifically to trap raptor species. Chicken wire is formed into a cage, with a floor of mesh welded wire, a lure entrance door and steel rod edging for ballast. The top is usually covered with fishing line. Pigeons, rats or mice can be used as lures for the four eagle-owls, each of which can then be exterminated. Tomorrow I shall draw a diagram and an outline of the mechanism for creating it. You will receive it by the midday post and your tiresome kennelboy should be able to build it easily enough. And now if you will excuse us, ladies.'

'Thank you for that advice, Sherlock,' said Irene Adler, leaning forward with difficulty in her chair. 'I was sure that you could help us. And I am sorry that you have to leave so soon. Violet, please arrange for a trap to take our heroes to the railway station in Norfolk.'

Before we took our leave, my curiosity got the better of me.

'What was the missing clue?' I asked.

'Oh, let me try to remember,' replied Irene Adler. 'It was: *City devastated by lair wobble.* Yes, that was it. Two words. Three letters, followed by nine.'

'***San Francisco***!' I cried in triumph.

'Why?' demanded Holmes.

'Well, the *lair* of a badger is an *earth*, and to *wobble* means to *quake*.'

'Let us be gone, Watson. Before you become any wiser. I am not at all sure that I could cope with that.'

We bade our farewells to the two ladies, my friend taking a tender moment with Irene Adler to mutter his final condolences.

Later that evening Holmes and I were back in Baker Street, discussing what had turned out to be a most unsatisfactory case.

'This has not been our best work, Watson,' he said wistfully. 'We should have realised that young master William would steam open the envelope to read its contents and then cut the bottom off to provide a spill for one of his cigarettes. You noticed the nicotine-stained fingers, of course?'

'No, I did not.'

'Oh, well. At least we can be thankful that there is no new Black Death,' sighed Holmes. 'It may be that we are getting too old for this game. Perhaps it is time for us to retire.'

'Nonsense!' I declared loyally.

'That's the spirit, old fellow! Look here, you can remind me of something. The elder Trevor made a rather interesting comment about ghosts all those years ago. Before being struck dead by the coded message he received, that is. What was it?'

'I remember. How could I forget? After all, I wrote the story. But I never understood it fully, and frankly it still puzzles me: *"Of all ghosts, the ghosts of our old loves are the worst."* '

WATCH OUT FOR:

1. *Sherlock Holmes And The Shepherds Bushman.*

2. *Sherlock Holmes And The Acton Body-Snatchers.*

3. *Sherlock Holmes And The Notting Hill Rapist.*

4. *Sherlock Holmes And The Clapham Witch.*

5. *Sherlock Holmes And The Battersea Fetishists.*

6. *Sherlock Holmes And The Kew Gardens Gnomes.*

7. *Sherlock Holmes And The Portobello Pornographer.*

8. *Sherlock Holmes And The Camden Counterfeiter.*

9. *Sherlock Holmes And The Kensington Kidnapper.*

10. *Sherlock Holmes And The Undiscovered Country.*

Also from MX Publishing

MX Publishing is the world's largest specialist Sherlock Holmes publisher, with over a hundred titles and fifty authors creating the latest in Sherlock Holmes fiction and non-fiction.

From traditional short stories and novels to travel guides and quiz books, MX Publishing cater for all Holmes fans.

The collection includes leading titles such as Benedict Cumberbatch In Transition and The Norwood Author which won the 2011 Howlett Award (Sherlock Holmes Book of the Year).

MX Publishing also has one of the largest communities of Holmes fans on Facebook with regular contributions from dozens of authors.

www.mxpublishing.com

Also from MX Publishing

After Mina Murray asks Sherlock Holmes to locate her fiancee, Holmes and Watson travel to a land far eerier than the moors they had known when pursuing the Hound of the Baskervilles. The confrontation with Count Dracula threatens Holmes' health, his sanity, and his life. Will Holmes survive his battle with Count Dracula?

www.mxpublishing.com

Also from MX Publishing

Internationally bestselling traditional short
story collections from Luke Kuhns

The Untold Adventures of Sherlock Holmes

Sherlock Holmes Studies In Legacy

www.mxpublishing.com

Also from MX Publishing

Dozens of short story ebooks

A lost chapter in the Holmes canon finally appears, as Dr. Watson recounts the mystery behind the tragic death of his beloved Mary Morstan. Join him as he attempts to bring a murderer to justice. Along the way, readers will encounter old friends and enemies from several of the other stories, leading to a startling conclusion that may baffle even Sherlock Holmes.

Available via Amazon Kindle, Kobo, Nook and iTunes.